FOR NOW

AND

FOREVER

(THE INN AT SUNSET HARBOR—BOOK 1)

SOPHIE LOVE

D1282503

ISBN: 978-1-63291-817-8

Chapter Two

Emily stared at her keyboard, willing her fingers to move, to do something, anything. Another email popped into her inbox and she looked at it blankly. The sound of the office chatter around her swirled in one ear and out the other. She couldn't concentrate. She felt like she was in a daze. The complete lack of sleep she'd gotten on Amy's lumpy couch was hardly helping matters.

She'd been at work a whole hour but hadn't achieved anything more than to turn on her computer and drink a cup of coffee. Her mind was completely consumed with memories of last night. Ben's face kept flashing through her head. It made her feel slightly panicked every time she relived the terrible evening.

Her phone began blinking, and she glanced at the screen to see Ben's name flashing at her for the umpteenth time. He was calling, again. She hadn't answered a single one of his calls. What could there possibly be to talk about now? He'd had seven years to work out whether he wanted to be with her or not—a last-minute attempt to save things wasn't going to do anything now.

Her office phone began to ring and she leapt a mile, then grabbed it.

"Hello?"

"Hi, Emily, it's Stacey from the fifteenth floor. I have it down that you were supposed to attend the meeting this morning and wanted to check in to see why you hadn't."

"SHIT!" Emily cried, slamming down the phone. She'd completely forgotten about the meeting.

She leapt up from her desk and ran across the office toward the elevator. Her frantic state seemed to amuse her co-workers, who began whispering like silly children. When she reached the elevator, she slammed her palm against the button.

"Come on, come on, come on!"

It took ages, but at last, the elevator arrived. As the doors slid open, Emily went to rush inside, only to slam straight into someone coming out. As she drew back, winded, she realized the person she'd slammed into was her boss, Izelda.

"I'm so sorry," Emily stammered.

Izelda looked her up and down. "For what, exactly? Slamming into me, or missing the meeting?"

"Both," Emily said. "I was on my way there right now. It completely slipped my mind."

She could feel every eye in the office burning into her back. The last thing she needed right now was a dose of public humiliation, something Izelda took great pleasure in dishing out.

"You have a calendar?" Izelda said coolly, folding her arms.

"Yes."

"And you know how it works? How to write?"

Behind Emily, she could hear people stifling their laughter. Her first instinct was to wilt like a flower. Being made a fool in front of an audience was her idea of a nightmare. But just like in the restaurant last night, a strange sense of clarity overcame her. Izelda wasn't some authority figure she had to look up to and bend to the whims of. She was just a bitter woman taking her anger out on anyone she could. And those colleagues whispering behind her back meant nothing.

A sudden wave of realization washed over Emily. Ben wasn't the only thing she didn't like about her life. She hated her job, too. These people, this office, Izelda. She'd been stuck here for years, just like she'd been stuck with Ben. And she wasn't going to put up with it anymore.

"Izelda," Emily said, addressing her boss by her first name for the first time ever, "I'm going to have to be honest here. I missed the meeting, it slipped my mind. It's not the worst thing in the world."

Izelda glowered.

"How dare you!" she snapped. "I'll have you working at your desk until midnight for the next month until you learn the value of being prompt!"

With those words Izelda brushed by her, bumping Emily's shoulder, as if to storm off, the matter clearly settled in her eyes.

But it wasn't settled in Emily's.

Emily reached out and grabbed Izelda's shoulder, stopping her.

Izelda turned and grimaced back, brushing Emily's hand off as if she'd been bitten by a snake.

But Emily did not give ground.

"I didn't finish," Emily continued, keeping her voice completely calm. "The worst thing in the world is this place. It's *you*. It's this stupid, petty, soul-destroying job."

"Excuse me?" Izelda cried, her face turning red with anger.

"You heard me," Emily replied. "In fact, I'm pretty sure *everyone* heard me."

Emily glanced over her shoulder at her colleagues, who stared back, dumbfounded. No one had expected quiet, compliant Emily to

5

snap like this. She recalled Ben's warning that she was "making a scene" last night. And here she was, making another one. Only this time she was enjoying it.

"You can take your job, Izelda," Emily added, "and stick it up your ass."

She could practically hear the gasps from behind her.

She shoved past Izelda into the elevator, then spun on her heel. She hit the ground floor button for what, she realized, with absolute relief, would be the last time in her life, then watched the scene of her stunned colleagues staring at her as the doors slid shut and blocked them out. She let out a huge sigh, feeling freer and lighter than she had ever felt.

*

Emily ran up the steps to her apartment, realizing it wasn't really her apartment—it never really had been. She'd always felt as if she were living in Ben's space, that she needed to make herself as small and unobtrusive as possible. She fumbled with her keys, grateful that he was at work and she wouldn't have to deal with him.

She got inside and looked at it with new eyes. Nothing in here was to her taste. Everything seemed to take on a new meaning; the horrible couch that she and Ben had argued over buying (an argument he won); the stupid coffee table that she wanted to throw out because one of the legs was shorter than the others and it always wobbled (but which Ben was attached to for "sentimental reasons" and so it stayed); the oversized TV that had cost far too much and took up too much space (but which Ben had insisted he needed in order to watch sports because it was the "only thing" that could keep him sane). She grabbed a couple of books from the shelf, noting how her romance novels had been relegated to the shadows of the bottom shelf (Ben was always worried their friends would think him less intellectual if they saw romance novels on the shelf—his preferences were academic texts and philosophers, although he never seemed to read any of them).

She glanced over the photos on the mantel to see if there was anything worth taking, when it struck her how every picture that contained her was with Ben's family. There they were at his niece's birthday, at his sister's wedding. There wasn't a single picture of her with her mom, the only person in her family, let alone of Ben spending any time with them both. It suddenly struck Emily that she

6

had been a stranger in her own life. She'd been following someone else's path for years rather than forging her own.

She stormed through the apartment and into the bathroom. Here were the only things that really mattered to her—her nice bath products and makeup. But even that was a problem for Ben. He'd constantly complained about how many products she had, lamenting on them being a waste of money.

"It's my money to waste!" Emily cried at her reflection in the mirror as she threw all her belongings into a tote bag.

She was aware that she looked like a madwoman, rushing around the bathroom throwing half-empty bottles of shampoo in her bag, but she didn't care. Her life with Ben had been nothing more than a lie, and she wanted to get out of it as quickly as possible.

She ran into the bedroom next and grabbed her suitcase from under the bed. She filled it quickly with all her clothes and shoes. Once she was done collecting her things, she dragged it all out into the street. Then, as a final symbolic gesture, she went back into the apartment and placed her key on Ben's "sentimental" coffee table, then left, never to return.

It was only as she stood on the curb that it really hit Emily what she had done. She had made herself jobless and homeless in the space of a few hours. Making herself single had been one thing, but chucking in her entire life was quite another.

Little flutters of panic began to race through her. Her hands trembled as she pulled out her cell and dialed Amy's number.

"Hey, what's up?" Amy said.

"I've done something crazy," Emily replied.

"Go on…" Amy urged her.

"I quit my job."

She heard Amy exhale on the other end of the line.

"Oh thank God," her friend's voice came. "I thought you were going to tell me you'd got back with Ben."

"No, no, quite the opposite. I packed my bags and left. I'm standing in the street like a bag lady."

Amy began to laugh. "I have the best mental image right now."

"This isn't funny!" Emily replied, more panicked than ever. "What am I supposed to do now? I quit my job. I won't be able to get an apartment without a job!"

"You've got to admit it's a bit funny," Amy replied, chuckling. "Just bring it all over here," she added, nonchalantly. "You know you can stay with me until you figure things out."

But Emily didn't want to. She'd essentially spent years of her life living in someone else's space, being made to feel like a lodger in her own home, like Ben was doing her a favor just by having her around. She didn't want that anymore. She needed to forge her own life, to stand on her own two feet.

"I appreciate the offer," Emily said, "but I need to do my own thing for a while."

"I get it," Amy replied. "So what then? Leave town for a bit? Clear your head?"

That got Emily thinking. Her dad owned a house in Maine. They'd stayed in it during the summer when she was a kid, but it had stayed empty ever since he'd disappeared twenty years ago. It was old, filled with character, and had been gorgeous at one point, in a historic sort of way; it had been more like a sprawling B&B that he didn't know what to do with than a house.

It was barely in passable shape back then, and Emily knew it wouldn't be in good shape now, after twenty years left derelict; it also wouldn't feel the same empty—or now that she wasn't a kid. Not to mention it was hardly summer. It was February!

And yet the idea of spending a few days just sitting on the porch, looking out at the ocean, in a place that was *hers* (sort of) seemed suddenly very romantic. Getting out of New York for the weekend would be a good way to clear her head and try to work out what to do next.

"I've got to go," Emily said.

"Wait," Amy replied. "Tell me where you're going first!"

Emily took a deep breath.

"I'm going to Maine."

Chapter Three

Emily had to take several subways to get to the long-term parking lot in Long Island City where her old, abandoned, beat-up car was parked. It had been years since she'd driven the thing, as Ben had always taken lead driver responsibilities in order to show off his precious Lexus, and as she walked through the massive, shadow-filled parking lot, dragging her suitcase behind her, she wondered whether she'd still be able to drive at all. It was another one of those thing she'd let slip over the course of her relationship.

The trip to get only here—to this parking lot on the outskirts of the city—felt endless. As she walked toward her car, her footsteps echoing in the freezing parking lot, she almost felt too tired to go on.

Was she making a mistake? she wondered. Should she turn back?

"There she is."

Emily turned to see the garage attendant smiling at her beat-up car, as if sympathetically. He reached out and dangled her keys.

The thought of still having an eight-hour drive ahead of her felt overwhelming, impossible. She was already exhausted, physically and emotionally.

"Are you going to take them?" he finally asked.

Emily blinked, not realizing she'd spaced out.

She stood there, knowing this was a pivotal moment somehow. Would she collapse, run back to her old life?

Or would she be strong enough to move on?

Emily finally shook off the dark thoughts and forced herself to be strong. At least for now.

She took the keys and walked triumphantly to her car, trying to show courage and confidence as he walked away, but secretly nervous that it would not even start—and if it did, that she would not even remember how to drive.

She sat in the freezing car, closed her eyes, and turned the ignition. If it started, she told herself, it was a sign. If it was dead, she could turn back.

She hated to admit it to herself, but she secretly hoped it would be dead.

She turned the key.

It started.

It came as a great surprise and comfort to Emily that, although a somewhat erratic driver, she still knew the basics of what she was doing. All she had to do was hit the gas and drive.

It was freeing, watching the world fly by, and slowly, she shook off her mood. She even turned on the radio, remembering it.

Radio blaring, windows rolled down, Emily gripped the steering wheel tightly in her hands. In her mind, she looked like a glamorous 1940s siren in a black-and-white film, with the wind tousling her perfectly coiffed hairstyle. In reality, the frigid February air had turned her nose as red as a berry and her hair into a frizzy mess.

She soon left the city, and the farther north she got, the more the roads became lined with evergreens. She gave herself time to admire their beauty as she whooshed past. How easily she'd let herself get caught up in the hustle and bustle of city living. How many years had she really let slide by without stopping to take in the beauty of nature?

Soon, the roads became wider, the number of lanes increasing, and she was on the highway. She revved the engine, pushing her beat-up car faster, feeling alive and enthralled by the speed. All these people in their cars embarking on journeys to elsewhere, and she, Emily, was finally one of them. Excitement pulsed through her as she urged the car onward, increasing her speed as much as she dared.

Her confidence soared as the roads flew by beneath her tires. As she passed through the state border into Connecticut, it really hit home that she was actually leaving. Her job, Ben, she'd finally discarded all that baggage.

The further north she went, the colder it became, and Emily finally had to concede that it was just too cold to have the window open. She buzzed it up and rubbed her hands together, wishing she was wearing something a little more appropriate for the weather. She'd left New York in her uncomfortable work suit, and in another moment of impulsivity, had flung the fitted jacket and stiletto shoes out the window. Now she was just in a thin shirt, and the toes of her bare feet seemed to have turned into frozen blocks of ice. The image of the 1940s movie star shattered in her mind as she glanced at her reflection in the rearview mirror. She looked a state. But she didn't care. She was free, and that was all that mattered.

Hours passed, and before she knew it, Connecticut was behind her, a distant memory, just a place she'd passed through on her way to a better future. The Massachusetts landscape was more open. Rather than the dark green foliage of evergreens, the trees here had shed their summer leaves and stood like spindly skeletons either side of her, revealing hints of snow and ice on the hard ground beneath them. Above Emily, the sky started to change color, from a clear blue to a muggy gray, reminding her that it was going to be dark by the time she reached Maine.

She drove through Worcester, many of the houses here tall, wood-paneled, and painted in various pastel shades. Emily couldn't help but wonder about the people who lived here, about their lives and experiences. She was only a few hours from home but already everything seemed alien to her—all the possibilities, all the different places to live and be and visit. How had she spent seven years living just one version of life, continuing the old, familiar routine, repeating the same day over and over, waiting, waiting, waiting for something more. All that time she'd been waiting for Ben to get his act together so she could begin the next chapter of her life. But all along, *she'd* had the power to be the driving force of her own story.

She found herself driving across a bridge, following Route 290 as it turned into Route 495. Gone were the trees to marvel at, replaced now by steep rock faces. Her stomach began to grumble, reminding her that lunch had come and gone and she'd done nothing about it. She considered stopping at a truck stop but the compulsion to get to Maine was too great. She could eat when she got there.

Hours more passed, and she crossed the state border into New Hampshire. The sky opened out, the roads wide and numerous, the plains stretching out either side of her as far as she could see. Emily couldn't help but think about how wide the world was, how many people it really contained.

Her sense of optimism carried her all the way past Portsmouth, where airplanes swooped over her, their engines rumbling as they approached the runway for landing. She sped on, past the next town, where frost covered the banks either side of the freeway, then onward through Portland, where the road ran alongside the train tracks. Emily took in every little detail, feeling awestruck by the size of the world.

She sped along the bridge that led out of Portland, wanting desperately to stop the car and take in the sight of the ocean. But the sky was growing darker and she knew she had to press on if she wanted to make it to Sunset Harbor before midnight. It was at least another three-hour drive from here, and the clock on her dashboard was already reading 9 p.m. Her stomach protested again, scolding her for having missed dinner as well as lunch.

Of all the things Emily was looking forward to the most when she arrived at the house, it was sleeping the night through. Fatigue was starting to set in; Amy's couch hadn't been particularly comfortable, not to mention the emotional turmoil Emily had been in all night. But waiting for her in the house in Sunset Harbor was the beautiful dark oak, four-poster bed that had been in the master bedroom, the one her parents had shared in happier times. The thought of having the whole thing to herself was compelling.

Despite the sky threatening snow, Emily decided against taking the highway all the way to Sunset Harbor. Her dad had been fond of driving the lesser-used route—a series of bridges spanning the myriad rivers running into the ocean around that part of Maine.

She exited the highway, relieved to at least slow her speed. The roads felt more treacherous, but the scenery was stunning. Emily gazed up at the stars as they blinked over the clear, sparkling water.

She stayed on Route 1 all along the coast, opening her mind to the beauty it had for her. The sky turned from gray to black, the water reflecting its image. It felt like she was driving through space, heading into infinity.

Heading toward the beginning of the rest of her life.

*

Weary from the endless drive, struggling to keep her raw eyes open, she perked up when her headlights finally lit up a sign that told her she was entering Sunset Harbor. Her heart beat quicker in relief and anticipation.

She passed the small airport and drove onto the bridge that would take her onto Mount Desert Island, remembering, with a pang of nostalgia, being in the family car as it raced over this very bridge. She knew it was only ten miles from here to the house, that it would take her no more than twenty minutes to reach her destination. Her heart started to hammer with excitement. Her fatigue and hunger seemed to disappear.

She saw the small wooden sign that welcomed her to Sunset Harbor and smiled to herself. Tall trees lined either side of the road, and Emily felt comforted to know they were the same trees she'd gazed out at as a child as her father drove along this very road.

A few minutes later she drove over a bridge she remembered strolling along as a child on a beautiful autumn evening, with red leaves crunching beneath her feet. The memory was so vivid she could even picture the purple woolen mittens she'd been wearing as she held hands with her father. She couldn't have been more than five at the time but the memory struck her as clearly as if it were yesterday.

More memories made their way into her mind as she passed other features—the restaurant that served awesome pancakes, the campground that would be filled with Scout groups all summer long, the single-track path that led down to Salisbury Cove. When she reached the sign for Acadia National Park she smiled, knowing she was just two miles from her final destination. It looked as though she was going to reach the house in the nick of time; snow was just starting to fall and her beat-up car probably didn't have it in it to get through a blizzard.

As if on cue, her car started emitting a strange grinding noise from somewhere beneath the hood. Emily bit her lip with anguish. Ben had always been the practical one, the tinkerer in the relationship. Her mechanical skills were woeful. She prayed the car would hold out for the last mile.

But the grinding noise got worse, and was soon accompanied by a strange whirr, then an irritating click, and finally a wheeze. Emily slammed her fists against the steering wheel and cursed under her breath. The snow began falling faster and thicker and her car started to complain even more, before it spluttered and finally ground to a halt.

Listening to the hiss of the dead engine, Emily sat there helplessly, trying to work out what to do. The clock told her it was midnight. There was no other traffic, no one out at this time of night. It was deathly quiet and, without her headlights to provide light, spectacularly dark; there were no street lamps on this road and clouds hid the stars and moon. It felt eerie, and Emily thought it was the perfect setting for a horror film.

She grabbed her phone like it was a comforter but saw there was no signal. The sight of those five empty bars of signal made her feel even more worried, even more isolated and alone. For the first time since up and leaving her life behind, Emily began to feel like she'd made a terribly stupid decision.

She got out of the car and shivered as the cold, snowy air bit at her flesh. She walked around to the trunk and took a look at the engine, not knowing what exactly she was even looking for.

Just then, she heard the rumbling of a truck. Her heart leapt with relief as she squinted into the distance and just about made out two headlights trundling along the road toward her. She began waving her arms, flagging the truck down as it approached.

Luckily, it pulled over, drawing to a halt just behind her car, sputtering exhaust fumes into the cold air, its harsh lights illuminating the falling snowflakes.

The driver's door creaked as it swung open, and two heavily booted feet crunched down into the snow. Emily could only see the silhouette of the person before her and had a sudden horrible panic that she'd flagged down the local murderer.

"Got yourself in a bad situation, have you?" she heard an old man's raspy voice say.

Emily rubbed her arms, feeling the goosebumps beneath her shirt, trying to stop herself from shivering—but relieved it was an old man.

"Yes, I don't know what happened," she said. "It started making strange noises then just stopped."

The man stepped closer, his face finally revealed by the lights of his truck. He was very old, with wiry white hair on his wrinkled face. His eyes were dark but sparkling with curiosity as he took in the sight of Emily, then the car.

"Don't know how it happened?" he asked, laughing under his breath. "I'll tell you how it happened. That car there is nothing more than a heap of junk. I'm surprised you even managed to drive it anywhere in the first place! Doesn't look like you've taken any care over it, then you decide to take it out in the snow?"

Emily wasn't in the mood to be mocked, especially since she knew the old man was right.

"Actually, I've come all the way from New York. It's held out fine for eight hours," she replied, failing to keep the dryness out of her tone.

The old man whistled under his breath. "New York? Well, I never… What brings you all this way?"

Emily didn't feel like divulging her story, so she just simply replied, "I'm heading to Sunset Harbor."

The man didn't question her further. Emily stood there watching him, her fingers quickly becoming numb as she waited for him to offer some kind of assistance. But he seemed more interested in pacing around her rusty old car, kicking its tires with the toe of his boot, flecking off the paint with a thumbnail, tutting and shaking his head. He opened the hood and examined the engine for a long, long time, muttering occasionally under his breath.

"So?" Emily said finally, exasperated by his slowness. "What's wrong with it?"

He looked up from the trunk, almost surprised, as though he'd forgotten she was even there, and scratched his head. "It's busted."

"I know that," Emily said, testily. "But can you do anything to fix it?"

"Oh no," the man replied, chuckling. "Not a thing."

Emily felt like screaming. The lack of food and the tiredness caused by the long drive were starting to affect her, making her close to the edge of tears. All she wanted was to get to the house so she could sleep.

"What am I going to do?" she said, feeling desperate.

"Well, you've got a couple of options," the old man replied. "Walk to the mechanic's, which is a mile or so that way." He pointed the way she'd come with one of his stubby, wrinkled fingers. "Or I could tow you to wherever it was you were heading."

"You would do that?" Emily said, surprised by his kindness, something she wasn't used to experiencing having lived in New York for so long.

"Of course," the man replied. "I'm not about to leave you out here at midnight in a snowstorm. Heard it was going to get worse in the next hour. Where is it exactly you're heading towards?"

Emily was overwhelmed with gratitude. "West Street. Number Fifteen."

The man cocked his head to the side with curiosity. "Fifteen West Street? That old, beat-up house?"

"Yes," Emily replied. "It belongs to my family. I needed to spend some quiet time to myself."

The old man shook his head. "I can't leave you at that place. The house is falling apart. I doubt it's even watertight. Why don't you come back to mine? We live above the convenience store, me and my wife, Bertha. We'd be happy to have a guest."

"That's very kind of you," Emily said. "But really I just want to be by myself at the moment. So if you could tow me to West Street I would really appreciate it."

The old man regarded her for a moment, then finally relented. "All right, missy. If you insist."

Emily felt a sense of relief as he got back in his truck and drove it in front of hers. She watched as he removed a thick rope from his trunk and tied their two vehicles together.

"Want to ride with me?" he asked. "At the very least I have heat."

Emily smiled thinly but shook her head. "I'd prefer to—"

"Be alone," the old man finished with her. "I get it. I get it."

Emily got back into her car, wondering what kind of impression she had made on the old man. He must be thinking she was a little mad, turning up underprepared and underdressed at midnight as a snowstorm was about to descend, demanding to be taken to a beat-up, abandoned house so she could be completely alone.

The truck ahead of her rumbled to life and she felt the pull as her car began to be towed. She sat back and glanced out the window as they moved off.

The road that carried her the last couple of miles ran beside the national park on one side and the ocean on the other. Through the darkness and a curtain of falling snow, Emily could see the ocean and the waves crashing against the rocks. Then the ocean disappeared from sight as they headed into the town, past hotels and motels, boat tour companies and golf courses, through the more built up areas, though for Emily it was hardly built up at all compared to New York.

Then they were turning onto West Street and Emily's heart lurched as they passed the grand red brick, ivy-covered house on the corner. It looked exactly the same as it had the last time she'd been here, twenty years earlier. She passed the blue house, the yellow house, the white house, and then she bit her lip, knowing the next house would be hers, the gray stone house.

As it appeared before her, Emily was struck by an overwhelming sense of nostalgia. The last time she'd been here she was fifteen years old, her body raging with hormones at the prospect of a summer romance. She'd never had one, but remembering the thrill of possibility hit her like a wave.

The truck pulled to a stop, and Emily's car did too.

Before the wheels had even finished turning, Emily was out, standing breathlessly before the house that had once been her father's. Her legs were shaking and she couldn't tell if it was from the relief of having finally arrived or the emotion of being back here after so many years. But where the other houses on the street seemed unchanged, her father's house was a shadow of its former glory. The once white window shutters were now streaked with dirt. Where once they'd stood open, all of them were closed up, making the house look far less inviting than it used to. The grass of the sweeping lawn out front where Emily had spent endless summer days reading novels was surprisingly well kept and the small shrubs either side of the front door were trimmed. But the house itself; she understood the old man's bemused expression now when she'd told him this was where she was heading. It looked so uncared for, so unloved, falling into disrepair. It made Emily sad to see how much the beautiful old house had decayed over the years.

"Nice house," the old man said as he drew up beside her.

"Thanks," Emily said, almost trancelike, with her eyes glued to the old building. Snow fluttered around her. "And thank you for getting me here in one piece," she added.

"No problem," the old man replied. "Are you really sure you want to stay here tonight?"

"I'm sure," Emily replied, though really she was starting to worry that coming here had been a huge mistake.

"Let me help you with your bags," the man said.

"No, no," Emily replied. "Honestly, you've done enough. I can take it from here." She rummaged in her pocket and found a crumpled bill. "Here, gas money."

The man looked at the note then back up at her. "I'm not taking that," he said, smiling kindly. "You keep your money. If you really want to pay me back, why don't you come down to mine and Bertha's some time during your stay and have some coffee and pie?"

Emily felt a lump form in her throat as she stashed the bill back in her pocket. This man's kindness was a shock to the system after the hostility of New York.

"How long are you planning on staying here anyway?" he added as he handed her a little slip of paper with a phone number and address scrawled on it.

"Just the weekend," Emily replied, taking the paper from him.

"Well, if you need anything, just give me a call. Or come to the gas station where I work. It's by the convenience store. Can't miss us."

"Thank you," Emily said again, with as much heartfelt gratitude as she could.

As soon as the noisy engine faded to nothing, the stillness descended over her again and Emily felt a sudden sense of peace.

The snow was falling even more now, making the world as silent as silent could be.

Emily returned to her car and grabbed her stuff, then waddled up the pathway with her heavy suitcase in her arms, feeling emotion rising in her chest. When she reached the front door she paused, examining the familiar worn doorknob, remembering her hand turning it a hundred times over. Maybe coming here had been a good idea after all. Oddly, she couldn't help but feel that she was exactly where she needed to be.

*

Emily stood in the dim hallway of her father's old house, dust swirling around her, stupidly hoping for warmth but rubbing her shoulders against the cold. She didn't know what she had been thinking. Had she really expected this old house, neglected for twenty years, to be waiting for her, heated?

She tried the light switch and found that nothing happened.

Of course, she realized. How stupid could she be? Did she expect the electricity to be on and running?

It hadn't even occurred to her to bring a flashlight. She chided herself. As usual, she had been too hasty and had not taken a moment to plan ahead.

She placed her suitcase down then paced forward, the floorboards creaking beneath her feet; she ran her fingertips along the swirly wallpaper just like she'd done as a little girl. She could even see the smudges she'd made over the years through that very motion. She passed the staircase, a long, wide set of steps in dark wood. It was missing part of the banister but she couldn't care less. Being back at the house felt beyond restorative.

She tried another light switch out of habit but again, no luck. Then she reached the door at the end of the hallway, which led into the kitchen, and pushed it open.

She gasped as a blast of freezing cold air hit her. She paced inside, the marble floor in the kitchen icy beneath her bare feet.

Emily tried turning the faucets in the sink but nothing happened. She chewed her lip in consternation. No heat, no electricity, no water. What else did the house have in store for her?

She paced around the house, looking for any switches or levers that might control the water, gas, and electricity. In the cupboard under the stairs she found a fuse box, but flicking the switches did nothing. The boiler, she remembered, was down in the basement—

but the idea of going down there without any light to lead the way filled her with trepidation. She needed a flashlight or candle, but knew there'd be nothing of the sort in the abandoned house. Still, she checked the kitchen drawers just in case—but they were just full of cutlery.

Panic began to flutter in Emily's chest and she willed herself to think. She cast her mind back to the times she and her family would spend at the house. She remembered the way her father used to arrange for oil to be delivered to heat the house during the winter months. It drove her mom crazy because it was so expensive and she thought heating an empty house was a waste of money. But Emily's father had insisted the house needed to be kept warm to protect the pipes.

Emily realized she needed to get some oil delivered if she wanted the house to be warm. But without a signal on her cell phone, she had no idea how she would make that happen.

All at once, there came a knock at the door. It was a heavy, steady, considered knock, one that echoed all the way through the empty corridors.

Emily froze, feeling a jolt of anticipation in her chest. Who could be calling, at this hour, in this snow?

She left the kitchen and padded across the hallway floorboards, silent with her bare feet. Her hand hovered over the knob, and after a second's hesitation, she managed to pull herself together and open the door.

Standing before her, wearing a plaid jacket, his dark, jaw-length hair peppered with snowflakes, stood a man who Emily couldn't help but think resembled a lumberjack, or Little Red Riding Hood's Huntsman. Not her usual type, but there was certainly beauty in his cool, blue eyes, in the stubble on his well-defined chin, and Emily was shocked by the power of her attraction toward him.

"Can I help you?" she asked.

The man squinted at her, as though sizing her up. "I'm Daniel," he said. He held out his hand for her to shake. She took it, noting the sensation of the rough skin of his hands. "Who are you?"

"Emily," she replied, suddenly aware of the sensation of her own heartbeat. "My father owns this house. I came for the weekend."

Daniel's squint intensified. "The landlord hasn't been here in twenty years. Did you get permission to just drop by?"

His tone was rough, slightly hostile, and Emily recoiled.

"No," she said, awkwardly, a little uncomfortable to be reminded of the most painful experience of her life—her father's disappearance—while being taken aback by Daniel's gruffness. "But I have his blessing to come and go as I please. What's it to you anyway?" She matched his rough tone with her own.

"I'm the caretaker here," he replied. "I live in the carriage house on the grounds."

"You *live* here?" Emily cried, her image of a peaceful weekend in her father's old home shattering before her. "But I wanted to be alone this weekend."

"Yeah, well, you and me both," Daniel replied. "I'm not used to people barging in unannounced." He glanced over her shoulder suspiciously. "And tampering with the property."

Emily folded her arms. "What makes you think I've tampered with the property?"

Daniel raised an eyebrow in response. "Well, unless you were planning on sitting here in the dark and cold all weekend, then I'd expect you to have tampered. Got the boiler running. Drained the pipes. That sort of thing."

Emily's gruffness gave way to embarrassment. She blushed.

"You haven't managed to get the boiler working, have you?" Daniel replied. There was a wry smile on his lips that told Emily he was slightly amused by her predicament.

"I just haven't had the chance to yet," she replied, haughtily, trying to save face.

"Want me to show you?" he asked, almost lazily, as though doing so would be no skin off his nose.

"You would?" Emily asked, a little shocked and confused by his offer to help.

He stepped onto the welcome mat. Snowflakes fluttered from his jacket, creating a mini snowstorm in the hallway.

"I'd prefer to do it myself than have you break something," he said by way of explanation, accompanied by a nonchalant shrug.

Emily noticed that the falling snow outside her open front door had turned into something of a blizzard. As much as she didn't want to admit it, she was beyond grateful that Daniel had shown up when he did. If not, she probably would have frozen to death overnight.

She shut the door and the two of them paced along the corridor to the door leading down to the basement. Daniel had come prepared. He pulled out a flashlight, lighting a path down the staircase into the basement. Emily followed him down, a little freaked out by the darkness and cobwebs as she descended into the gloom. She'd been terrified of the old basement as a child and had rarely ventured down there. The place was filled with all the old-fashioned machinery and mechanicals that kept the house working. The sight of them overwhelmed her and made her wonder once again whether coming here had been a mistake.

Thankfully, Daniel started the boiler up in a matter of seconds, as if it was the easiest thing in the world. Emily couldn't help but feel a little put out by the fact she'd needed a man to help her when the very reason she'd come here in the first place was to regain her independence. She realized then that despite Daniel's rugged hotness and her undeniable attraction toward him, she needed him to leave ASAP. She was hardly going to go on a journey of self-discovery with him in the house. Having him on the grounds was bad enough.

Finished with the boiler, they both left the basement. Emily was relieved to be out of the dank, musty place and back into the main part of the house. She followed Daniel as he went down the hall and into the utility room out the back of the kitchen. Straightaway he got to work draining the pipes.

"Are you prepared to heat the house all winter?" he called to her from his position under the worktop. "Because they'll freeze otherwise."

"I'm just staying for the weekend," Emily replied.

Daniel shuffled out from under the counter and sat up, his hair ruffled and sticking up all over the place. "You shouldn't mess with an old house like this," he said, shaking his head.

But he sorted out the water nonetheless.

"So where's the heat?" Emily asked as soon as he was done. It was still freezing cold, despite the boiler being on and the pipes now unblocked. She rubbed her arms, trying to get the circulation going.

Daniel laughed, cleaning his dirty hands on a towel. "It doesn't just miraculously start working, you know. You'll need to call for oil delivery. All I could do is start the thing up."

Emily sighed with frustration. So Daniel wasn't quite the Knight in Shining Armor she thought he was.

"Here," Daniel said, handing her a business card. "That's Eric's number. He'll deliver to you."

"Thanks," she mumbled. "But I don't seem to get service out here."

She thought of her cell phone, of the empty bars, and remembered how wholly alone she really was.

21

"There's a pay phone up the road," Daniel said. "But I wouldn't risk going there in the middle of a blizzard. And anyway, they'll be closed now."

"Of course," Emily mumbled, feeling frustrated and completely at a loss.

Daniel must have noticed that Emily was put out and feeling dejected. "I can get a fire going for you," he offered, nodding toward the living room. His eyebrows rose expectantly, almost shyly, making him look suddenly boyish.

Emily wanted to protest, to tell him to leave her alone in the freezing cold house because that's the least she deserved, but something made her hesitate. Perhaps it was that having Daniel in the house made her feel suddenly less lonely, less cut off from civilization. She hadn't expected to have no cell phone service, no ability to communicate with Amy, and the reality of spending her first night alone in the cold, dark house was daunting.

Daniel must have read into her hesitation because he strode out of the room before she got a chance to open her mouth and say anything.

She followed, silently grateful that he'd been able to read the loneliness in her eyes and had offered to remain, even if it was under the guise of starting a fire. She found Daniel in the living room, busy constructing a neat pile of kindling, coal, and logs in the fireplace. She was struck immediately with a memory of her father, of him crouched by the fireplace expertly creating fires, spending as much care and time over them as someone might a great work of art. She'd watched him make a thousand of them, and had always loved them. She found fires hypnotic and would spend hours stretched out on the rug before them, watching the orange and red flames dance, sitting for so long the heat would sting her face.

Emotion began to creep up Emily's gullet, threatening to choke her. Thinking of her father, seeing so clearly the memory in her mind, made long suppressed tears well in her eyes. She didn't want to cry in front of Daniel, didn't want to look like a pathetic, helpless damsel. So she balled her emotions up inside and strode purposefully into the room.

"I actually know how to make a fire," she said to Daniel.

"Oh, you do?" Daniel replied, looking up at her with a cocked eyebrow. "Be my guest." He held out the matches.

Emily snatched them up and struck one alight, the little orange flame flickering in her fingers. The truth was, she'd only ever watched her father making fires; she herself had never actually made one. But she could see so vividly in her memory how to do it that she felt confident in her ability. So she knelt down and set fire to the bits of kindling Daniel had place at the bottom of the fireplace. In a matter of seconds the fire went up, making a familiar *whomp* that felt as comforting and nostalgic to her as anything else the great house contained. She felt very proud of herself as the flames began to grow. But instead of going up the chimney, black smoke started billowing into the room.

"SHIT!" Emily cried as plumes of smoke billowed around her.

Daniel started laughing. "Thought you said you knew how to make a fire," he said, opening the flue. The plume of smoke was immediately sucked up into the chimney. "Ta-da," he added with a grin.

As the smoke around them thinned out, Emily gave him a displeased look, too proud to thank him for the help she'd so clearly needed. But she was relieved to finally be warm. She felt her circulation kick in, and the warmth returned to her toes and nose. Her stiff fingers loosened.

In the firelight, the living room was illuminated and bathed in a soft, orange light. Emily could finally see all the old antique furniture her dad had filled the house with. She glanced around her at the shabby, uncared for items. The tall bookcase stood in one corner, once crammed full of books that she'd spent her endless summer days reading, now with just a few remaining. Then there was the old grand piano by the window. No doubt it would be out of tune by now, but once upon a time, her father would play her songs and she would sing along. Her father had taken such great pride in the house, and seeing it now, the glowing light revealing its unkempt state, upset her.

The two couches were covered with white sheets. Emily thought about removing them but knew it would cause a dust cloud. After the smoke cloud, she wasn't sure her lungs could take it. And anyway, Daniel looked pretty cozy sitting on the floor beside the fireplace, so she just settled down beside him.

"So," Daniel said, warming his hands against the fire. "We've got you some warmth at the very least. But there's no electricity in the house and I'm guessing you didn't think to pack a lantern or candle in that suitcase of yours."

Emily shook her head. Her suitcase was filled with frivolous things, nothing useful, nothing she'd really need to get by here.

"Dad used to always have candles and matches," she said. "He was always prepared. I suppose I expected there to still be a whole cupboard full, but after twenty years..."

She shut her mouth, suddenly aware of having articulated a memory of her father aloud. It wasn't something she did often, usually keeping her feelings about him hidden deeply inside of her. The ease with which she'd spoken of him shocked her.

"We can just stay in here then," Daniel said gently, as though recognizing that Emily was re-experiencing some painful memory. "There's plenty of light to see by with the fire. Want some tea?"

Emily frowned. "Tea? How exactly are you going to do that without any electricity?"

Daniel smiled as though accepting some kind of challenge. "Watch and learn."

He stood up and disappeared from the vast living room, returning a few minutes later with a small round pot that looked like a cauldron.

"What have you got there?" Emily asked, curious.

"Oh, just the best tea you're ever going to drink," he said, placing the cauldron over the flames. "You've never had tea 'til you've had fire-boiled tea."

Emily watched him, the way the firelight danced off his features, accentuating them in a way that made him even more attractive. The way he was so focused on his task added to the appeal. Emily couldn't help but marvel at his practicality, his resourcefulness.

"Here," he said, handing her a cup and breaking through her reverie. He watched expectantly as she took the first sip.

"Oh, that's really good," Emily said, relieved, at last, to be banishing the cold from her bones.

Daniel started to laugh.

"What?" Emily challenged him.

"I just hadn't seen you smile yet, is all," he replied.

Emily looked away, feeling suddenly bashful. Daniel was about as far away from Ben as a man could be, and yet her attraction toward him was powerful. Maybe in another place, another time, she'd give in to her lust. She'd been with no one but Ben for seven years, after all, and she deserved some attention, some excitement.

But now wasn't the right time. Not with everything going on, with her life in complete chaos and upheaval, and with the memories of her father swirling round in her mind. She felt that everywhere she looked, she could see the shadows of him; sitting on the sofa with a young Emily curled into his side, reading to her aloud; bursting in through the door beaming from ear to ear after discovering some precious antique at the flea market, then spending hours carefully cleaning it, restoring it to its former glory. Where were all the antiques now? All the figurines and artwork, the commemorative crockery and Civil War–era cutlery pieces? The house hadn't stood still, frozen in time, like it had in her memory. Time had taken its toll on the property in a way she hadn't even considered.

Another wave of grief crashed over Emily as she glanced around at the dusty, disheveled room that had once been brimming with life and laughter.

"How did this place get into this state?" she suddenly cried, unable to keep the accusatory tone out of her voice. She frowned. "I mean, you're supposed to be taking care of it, aren't you?"

Daniel flinched, as though taken aback by her sudden aggressiveness. Just moments earlier they'd shared a gentle, tender moment. Seconds later she was giving him a hard time. Daniel flashed her a cool stare. "I do my best. It's a big house. There's only one of me."

"Sorry," Emily said, immediately backtracking, not liking to be the cause of Daniel's darkened expression one bit. "I didn't mean to take a dig at you. I just mean…" She looked into her cup and swirled the tea leaves. "This place was like something out of a fairytale when I was a kid. It was so awe-inspiring, you know? So beautiful." She looked up to see Daniel watching her intently. "It's just sad to see it like this."

"What were you expecting?" Daniel replied. "It's been abandoned for twenty years."

Emily looked away sadly. "I know. I guess I just wanted to imagine that it had been suspended in time."

Suspended in time, like the image of her father that she had in her mind. He was still forty years old, never having aged a day, looking identical to the last time she'd seen him. But wherever he was, time would have affected him just like it had affected the house. Emily's resolve to fix up the house over the weekend grew even stronger. She wanted nothing more than to restore the place, if only slightly, back to its old glory. Maybe in doing so, it would be like bringing her father back to her. She could do it in his honor.

Emily took her last sip of tea and set the cup down. "I should get to bed," she said. "It's been a long day."

"Of course," Daniel replied, standing. He moved quickly, waltzing out of the room and down the corridor toward the front door, leaving Emily to tag along behind. "Just call on me when you find yourself in trouble, okay?" he added. "I'm just in the carriage house over there."

"I won't need to," Emily said indignantly. "I can do it myself."

Daniel hauled open the front door, letting the bracing snow swirl inside. He hunkered down in his jacket, then looked back over his shoulder. "Pride won't get you far in this place, Emily. There's nothing wrong with asking for help."

She wanted to shout something at him, to argue, to refute his claim that she was too proud, but instead she watched his back as he disappeared into the dark, swirling snow, unable to speak, her tongue completely tied.

Emily closed the door, shutting out the outside world and the fury of the blizzard. She was now completely alone. Light spilled into the hallway from the living room fire but wasn't strong enough to reach up the stairs. She glanced up the long, wooden staircase as it disappeared into blackness. Unless she was prepared to sleep on one of the dusty couches, she would have to get the nerve to venture upstairs and into the pitch-blackness. She felt like a child again, scared of descending into the shadow-filled basement, inventing all kinds of monsters and ghouls that were waiting down there to get her. Only now she was a grown woman of thirty-five, too scared to go upstairs because she knew the sight of abandonment was worse than any ghoul her mind could create.

Instead, Emily went back into the living room to soak up the last of the warmth from the fire. There were still a few books on the bookshelf—*The Secret Garden, Five Children, It*—classics her father had read to her. But what of the rest? Where had her father's belongings gone? They had disappeared into that unknown place just like her father had.

As the embers began to die, darkness settled in around her, matching her somber mood. She could put off the fatigue no longer; the time had come to climb the steps.

Just as she left the living room, she heard a strange scratching noise coming from the front door. Her first thought was some kind of wild creature sniffing around for scraps, but the noise was too precise, too considered.

Heart pounding, she padded along the hall on silent feet and drew up to the front door, pressing her ear against it. Whatever she thought she'd heard, it was gone now. All she could hear was the screaming wind. But something compelled her to open the door.

She pulled it open and saw that placed on the doorstep were candles, a lantern, and matches. Daniel must have come back and left them for her.

She snatched them up, grudgingly accepting his offer of help, her pride stung. But at the same time she was beyond grateful that there was someone looking out for her. She might have given up her life and run away to this place, but she wasn't completely alone here.

Emily lit the lantern and finally felt brave enough to go upstairs. As the soft lantern light led her up the staircase, she took in the sight of the picture frames on the wall, the images inside them faded with time, the cobwebs strung across them covered in dust. Most of the pictures were watercolors of the local area—sailing boats on the ocean, evergreens in the national park—but one was a family portrait. She stopped, staring at the picture, looking at the image of herself as a little girl. She had completely forgotten about this picture, had confined it to some part of her memory and locked it away for twenty years.

Swallowing her emotion, she continued to climb the steps. The old stairs creaked loudly beneath her and she noticed that some of the steps had cracked. They were scuffed from years of footsteps and a memory struck her of running up and down these steps in her red T-bar shoes.

Up in the hallway the lantern light illuminated the long corridor—the numerous dark-oak wood doors, the floor-to-ceiling window at the end that was now boarded up. Her old bedroom was the last on the right, opposite the bathroom. She couldn't bear the thought of looking in either room. Too many memories would be contained in her bedroom, too many for her to unleash right now. And she didn't much fancy finding out what kind of creepy crawlies had made the bathroom their home over the years.

Instead, Emily stumbled along the corridor, weaving past the antique ornament case she'd stubbed her toe on countless times, and into her parents' room.

In the lantern light, Emily could see how dusty the bed was, how moth-bitten the bedding had become over the years. The memory of the beautiful four-poster bed that her parents had shared shattered in her mind as she was confronted with the reality. Twenty years of abandonment had ravaged the room. The curtains were grimy and crumpled, hanging limply beside the boarded up windows. The wall sconces were thick with dust and cobwebs, looking like whole generations of spider families had made them home. A layer of thick dust had settled over everything, including the dressing table beside the window, the little stool her mother had sat upon many years ago as she'd lathered her face with lavender-scented cream in the vanity mirror.

Emily could see it all, all the memories she had buried over the years. She couldn't help the tears from coming. All the emotions she'd felt over the last few days caught up with her, intensified by thoughts of her father, of the sudden shock of how much she missed him.

Outside, the sound of the blizzard intensified. Emily set the lantern down on the bedside table, sending a cloud of dust into the air as she did so, and readied herself for bed. The warmth of the fire hadn't reached this far up and the room was bitingly cold as she removed her clothes. In her suitcase she found her silky camisole and realized it wasn't going to be much use to her here; she would be better off with unflattering long johns and thick bed socks.

Emily pulled back the dusty crimson and gold patchwork cover then slid into the bed. She stared up at the ceiling for a moment, reflecting on everything that had happened over the last few days. Lonely, cold, and feeling helpless, she blew out the flame of the lantern, plunging herself into darkness, and cried herself to sleep.

Chapter Four

Emily woke early the next morning feeling disorientated. There was such little light coming into the room from the boarded-up windows, it took her a moment to realize where she was. Her eyes slowly adjusted to the dimness, the room materialized around her, and she remembered—Sunset Harbor. Her father's home.

A moment went by before she remembered that she was also jobless, homeless, and completely alone.

She dragged her weary body out of bed. The morning air was cold. Her appearance in the dusty vanity mirror alarmed her; her face was puffy from the tears she'd shed the night before, her skin drawn and pale. It suddenly occurred to her that she'd failed to eat sufficiently the previous day. The only thing she'd consumed the night before had been a cup of Daniel's fire-brewed tea.

She hesitated momentarily beside the mirror, looking at her body reflected in the old, grimy glass while her mind played over the night before—of the warming fire, of her sitting by the hearth with Daniel drinking tea, Daniel mocking her inability to care for the house. She remembered the snow flecks in his hair when she'd first opened the door to him, and the way he'd retreated into the blizzard, disappearing into the inky black night as quickly as he'd come.

Her growling stomach dragged her out of her thoughts and back into the moment. She dressed quickly. The crumpled shirt she pulled on was far too thin for the cold air so she wrapped the dusty blanket from the bed around her shoulders. Then she left the bedroom and padded downstairs on bare feet.

Downstairs, all was silent. She peered through the frosted window in the front door and was astonished to see that although the storm had now stopped, snow was piled three feet high, turning the world outside into a smooth, still, endless whiteness. She had never seen that much snow in her life.

Emily could just make out the footprints of a bird as it had hopped around on the path outside, but other than that, nothing had been disturbed. It looked peaceful, but at the same time desolate, reminding Emily of her loneliness.

Realizing that venturing outside wasn't an option, Emily decided to explore the house and see what, if anything, it might hold. The house had been so dark last night she hadn't been able to look around too much, but now in the morning daylight the task was somewhat easier. She went into the kitchen first, driven instinctively by her grumbling stomach.

The kitchen was in more of a state than she'd realized when she'd wandered through here last night. The fridge—an original cream 1950s Prestcold her father had found during a yard sale one summer—wasn't working. She tried to remember whether it ever had, or whether it had been another source of annoyance for her mother, another one of those bits of junk her dad had cluttered the old house up with. Emily had found her dad's collections boring as a kid, but now she treasured those memories, clinging onto them as tightly as she could.

Inside the fridge Emily found nothing but a horrible smell. She shut it quickly, locking the door with the handle, before going over to the cupboards to look inside. Here she found an old can of corn, its label sun-bleached to the point of obscurity, and a bottle of malt vinegar. She briefly considered making some kind of meal out of the items but decided she wasn't yet that desperate. The can opener was rusted completely closed anyway, so there'd be no way to get into the corn even if she was.

She went into the pantry next, where the washer and dryer were located. The room was dark, the small window covered with plywood like many of the others in the house. Emily pressed a button on the washer dryer but wasn't surprised to find that it didn't work. Growing increasingly frustrated with her situation, Emily decided to take action. She clambered up onto the sideboard and attempted to pry off a piece of plywood. It was harder to do than she'd expected, but she was determined. She pulled and pulled, using all the force in her arms. Finally, the board began to crack. Emily wrenched one last time and the plywood gave, coming away from the window entirely. The force was so great she fell back off the counter, the heavy board falling from her grasp and swinging toward the window. Emily heard the sound of the window smashing at the same time as she landed on a heap on the floor, winding herself.

Frigid air rushed into the pantry. Emily groaned and pulled herself up to sitting before checking her bruised body to make sure nothing was broken. Her back was sore and she rubbed it as she glanced up at the broken window letting in a weak stream of light. It frustrated Emily to realize that in attempting to solve a problem, she'd only made things worse for herself.

She took a deep breath and stood, then carefully picked up the piece of board from the sideboard where it had fallen. Bits of glass fell to the ground and smashed. Emily inspected the board and saw that the nails were completely bent. Even if she were able to find a hammer—something she strongly doubted—the nails would be too bent anyway. Then she saw that she'd managed to split the frame of the window while yanking the board off. The whole thing would need to be replaced.

Emily was far too cold to stand around in the pantry. Through the smashed window she was confronted by the same sight of endless white snow. She snatched her blanket up off the floor and secured it around her shoulders again, then left the pantry and headed into the living room. At least here she'd be able to light a fire and get some warmth into her bones.

In the living room, the comforting smell of burnt wood still lingered in the air. Emily crouched beside the fireplace and began stacking kindling and logs into a pyramid shape. This time, she remembered to open the flue, and was relieved when the first flame crackled to life.

She sat back on her heels and began to warm her cold hands. Then she noticed the pot that Daniel had brewed the tea in sitting next to the fireplace. She hadn't tidied anything up, and the pot and mugs still lay where they'd left them the night before. Memories flashed in her mind of her and Daniel sharing the tea, chatting about the old house. Her stomach growled, reminding her of her hunger, and she decided to brew some tea just like Daniel had shown her, reasoning that it would stave off her hunger for a little while at least.

Just as she had finished setting the pot up over the fire, she heard the sound of her phone ringing from somewhere in the house. Though a familiar noise, it made her jump a mile to hear it now, echoing through the corridors. She'd given up on it when she realized she had no signal, so the sound of its ring was a surprise to her.

Emily leapt up, abandoning the tea, and followed the sound of her phone. She found it on the cabinet in the hallway. An unfamiliar number was calling her and she answered, somewhat bemused.

"Oh, um, hi," the elderly male voice on the other end of the line said. "Are you the lady up at Fifteen West Street?" The line was bad and the man's soft, hesitant voice was almost inaudible.

Emily frowned, confused by the call. "Yes. Who is this?"

"The name's Eric. I, er, I deliver the oil to all the properties in the area. I heard you were staying at that old house so I thought I'd come over with a delivery. I mean, if you, uh, need it."

Emily could hardly believe it. News had certainly gotten around the small community quickly. But wait; how had Eric gotten her cell number? Then she remembered Daniel looking at it the night before when she told him she had spotty service. He must have seen the number and memorized it, planning to give it to Eric. So much for being prideful, she could hardly contain her delight.

"Yes, that would be wonderful," she replied. "When can you come?"

"Well," the man replied in the same nervous, almost embarrassed-sounding voice. "I'm actually in the truck now heading over there."

"You are?" Emily stammered, hardly believing her luck. She peered quickly at the time on her phone. It wasn't even 8 a.m. yet. Either Eric got to work super early as a matter of course or he'd made the trip especially for her. She wondered whether the man who'd given her a lift last night had gotten in touch with the oil company on her behalf. Either it was him or... Daniel?

She put the thought out of her mind and returned her attention to her telephone conversation. "Will you be able to get here?" she asked. "There's a lot of snow."

"Don't worry about that," Eric said. "The truck can handle snow. Just make sure a pathway is clear to the pipe."

Emily wracked her brain, trying to remember whether she'd seen a shovel anywhere in the house. "Okay, I'll do my best. Thank you."

The line went dead and Emily sprang into action. She raced back into the kitchen, checking each of the cupboards. There was nothing even close to what she needed, so she tried all the cupboards in the pantry, then on into the utility room. At last, she found a snow shovel propped up against the back door. Emily never thought she'd be so thrilled to see a shovel in all her life, but she grabbed hold of it like a lifeline. She was so excited about the shovel that she almost forgot to put any shoes on. But just as her hand hovered over the latch to open the back door, she saw her running sneakers sticking out of a bag she'd left there. She put them on quickly then yanked the door open, her precious shovel in her grasp.

Immediately, the depth and scale of the snowstorm became apparent to her. Looking out at the snow from her window had been one thing, but seeing it piled up three feet deep ahead of her like a wall of ice was another.

Emily wasted no time. She slammed the shovel into the wall of snow and ice and began to carve a path out of the house. It was hard going; within a matter of minutes she could feel the sweat dripping down her back, her arms ached, and she was certain that she'd have blisters on her palms once she was done.

After getting through three feet of snow, Emily began to find her rhythm. There was something cathartic about the task, about the momentum needed to shovel the snow. Even the physical unpleasantness seemed to matter less when she could begin to see how her efforts were being rewarded. Back in New York her favorite form of exercise was running on the treadmill, but this was more of a workout than any she'd had before.

Emily managed to carve out a ten-foot-long path through the grounds at the back of the house.

But she looked up in despair to see the pipe outlet was a good forty feet away—and she was already spent.

Trying not to despair too much, she decided to rest for a moment to catch her breath. As she did so, she caught sight of the caretaker's house farther along the garden, hidden beside evergreens. A small plume of smoke rose from the chimney and warm light spilled from the windows. Emily couldn't help but think of Daniel inside, drinking his tea, staying toasty warm. He would help her, she had no doubt about that, but she wanted to prove herself. He'd mocked her mercilessly the evening before, and had in all likelihood been the one to call Eric in the first place. He must have perceived her to be a damsel in distress, and Emily didn't want him to have the satisfaction of being proved right.

But her stomach was complaining again and she was exhausted. Far too exhausted to carry on. Emily stood in the river she'd created, suddenly overwhelmed by her predicament, too proud to call for the help she needed, too weak to do what needed to be done herself. Frustration mounted inside of her until it turned to hot tears. Her tears made her even more angry, angry at herself for being useless. In her frustrated mind, she berated herself and, like a petulant and stubborn child, resolved to return home as soon as the snow had melted.

Discarding the shovel, Emily stomped back into the house, her sneakers soaked through. She kicked them off by the door then went back into the living room to warm up by the fire.

She slumped down onto the dusty couch and grabbed her phone, preparing herself to call Amy and tell her the oh-so-expected news that she'd failed her first and only attempt at being self-sufficient. But the phone was out of battery. Stifling a screech, Emily threw her useless cell back onto the couch, then flopped onto her side, utterly defeated.

Through her sobbing, Emily heard a scraping noise coming from outside. She sat up, dried her eyes, then ran to the window and looked out. Right away she saw that Daniel was there, her discarded shovel in his grasp, digging through the snow and continuing what she had failed to complete. She could hardly believe how quickly he was able to clear the snow, how adept he was, how well suited to the task at hand, like he had been born to work the land. But her admiration was short-lived. Instead of feeling grateful toward Daniel or pleased to see that he had managed to clear a path all the way to the outlet pipe, she felt angry with him, directing her own impotence at him instead of inwardly.

Without even thinking about what she was doing, Emily grabbed her soggy sneakers and heaved them back on. Her mind was racing with thoughts; memories of all her useless ex-boyfriends who hadn't listened to her, who'd stepped in and tried to "save" her. It wasn't just Ben; before him had been Adrian, who was so overprotective he was stifling, and then there was Mark before him, who treated her like a fragile ornament. Each of them had learned of her past—her father's mysterious disappearance being just the tip of the iceberg—and had treated her like something that needed protecting. It was all those men in her past who had made her this way and she wasn't going to stand for it anymore.

She stormed out into the snow.

"Hey!" she cried. "What are you doing?"

Daniel paused only briefly. He didn't even look back over his shoulder at her, just kept on shoveling, before calmly saying, "I'm clearing a path."

"I can see that," Emily shot back. "What I mean is why, when I told you I didn't need your help?"

"Because otherwise you'd freeze," Daniel replied simply, still not looking at her. "And so would the water, now that I've turned it on."

"So?" Emily retorted. "What's it to you if I freeze? It's my life. I can freeze if I want to."

Daniel was in no hurry to interact with Emily, or feed into the argument she was so clearly trying to start. He just kept on shoveling, calmly, methodically, as unrattled by her presence as he would have been if she hadn't been there at all.

"I'm not prepared to sit back and let you die," Daniel replied.

Emily folded her arms. "I think that's a little bit melodramatic, don't you? There's a big difference between getting a bit cold and dying!"

Finally, Daniel rammed the shovel into the snow and straightened up. He met her eyes, his expression unreadable. "That snow was piled so high it was covering the exhaust. You manage to get that boiler on, it would go right back into the house. You'd be dead of carbon poisoning in about twenty minutes." He said it so matter-of-factly it took Emily aback. "If you want to die, do it on your own time. But it's not happening on my watch." Then he threw the shovel to the ground and headed back to the carriage house.

Emily stood there, watching him going, feeling her anger melt away only to be replaced with shame. She felt terrible for the way she'd spoken to Daniel. He was only trying to help and she'd thrown it all back in his face like a bratty child.

She was tempted to run to him, to apologize, but at that moment the oil truck appeared at the end of the street. Emily felt her heart soar, surprised at how happy she felt by the mere fact that she was getting oil delivered. Being in the house in Maine was about as different from her life in New York as it could be.

Emily watched as Eric leapt down from the truck, surprisingly agile for someone so old. He was dressed in oil-stained overalls like a character from a cartoon. His face was weather-beaten but kindly.

"Hi," he said in the same unsure manner he'd had on the phone.

"I'm Emily," Emily said, offering her hand to shake his. "I'm really glad you're here."

Eric just nodded, and got straight to work setting up the oil pump. He clearly wasn't one for talking, and Emily stood there uncomfortably watching him work, smiling weakly every time she noticed his gaze flick briefly to her as though confused by the fact she was even there.

"Can you show me to the boiler?" he said once everything was in place.

Emily thought of the basement, of her hatred of the huge machines within it that powered the house, of the thousands of spiders who'd strung their webs there throughout the years.

"Yes, this way," she replied in a small, thin voice.

Eric got out his flashlight and together they went down into the creepy, dark basement. Just like Daniel, Eric seemed to have a skilled hand with the mechanical stuff. Within seconds, the enormous boiler kicked into life. Emily couldn't help herself; she threw her arms around the elderly man.

"It works! I can't believe it works!"

Eric stiffened at her touch. "Well, you shouldn't be messing with an old house like this," he replied.

Emily loosened her grip. She didn't even care that yet another person was telling her to stop, to give up, that she wasn't good enough. The house now had heat along with water, and that meant she didn't need to return to New York as a failure.

"Here," Emily said, grabbing her purse. "How much do I owe you?"

Eric just shook his head. "It's all covered," he replied.

"Covered by who?" Emily asked.

"Just someone," Eric replied evasively. He clearly felt uncomfortable being caught up in the unusual situation. Whoever had paid him to come over and stock up her oil supply must have asked him to keep it quiet and the whole situation was making him awkward.

"Well, okay," Emily said. "If you say so."

Inwardly she resolved to find out who had done it, and to pay him back.

Eric just nodded once, sharply, then headed back up out of the basement. Emily quickly followed, not wanting to be in the basement alone. As she climbed the steps, she noticed she had a renewed spring in her step.

She showed Eric to the door.

"Thank you, really," she said as meaningfully as she could.

Eric said nothing, just gave her a parting look, then headed outside to pack up his things.

Emily shut the door. Feeling elated, she rushed upstairs to the master bedroom and put her hand against the radiator. Sure enough, warmth was beginning to spread through the pipes. She was so happy she didn't even mind the way they banged and clanked, the noise echoing through the house.

*

As the day wore on, Emily reveled in the sensation of being warm. She hadn't fully realized how uncomfortable she'd been ever since leaving New York, and hoped that some of the crabbiness she'd thrown at Daniel had been in part because of that discomfort.

No longer needing the dusty blanket from the master bedroom for warmth, Emily draped it over the broken window in the pantry before setting about cleaning up the glass fragments. She hung her wet clothes over the radiators, beat the dust out of the rug in the living room, and dusted all the shelves before setting the books up neatly. Already the room felt cozier, and more like the place she remembered. She took down her old, well-read copy of *Alice Through The Looking Glass*, then set about reading it by the hearth. But she couldn't concentrate. Her mind continually wandered back to Daniel. She felt so ashamed of the way she'd treated him. Though he acted as though he didn't care, the way he'd thrown the shovel and stormed back to the house was evidence enough that her words had frustrated him.

The guilt gnawed at her until she couldn't take it anymore. She abandoned the book, put on her now toasty warm sneakers, and headed out toward the carriage house.

She knocked on the door and waited as the sound of someone moving about came from inside. Then the door swung open and there was Daniel, backlit by the glow of a warm fire. A delicious smell wafted out of the house, reminding Emily again that she hadn't eaten. She began to salivate.

"What's up?" Daniel asked, his tone as measured as always.

Emily couldn't help but peer over his shoulder, taking in the sight of the roaring fire, the varnished floorboards and crammed bookshelves, the guitar propped up beside a piano. She hadn't known what to expect from Daniel's home, but it hadn't been this. The incongruity of the place in which Daniel lived and the person she'd assumed him to be surprised her.

"I was…" she stammered. "Just here to…" Her voice trailed away.

"Here to ask for some soup?" Daniel suggested.

Emily snapped to attention. "No. Why would you think that?"

Daniel gave her a look that was a cross between amused and reproachful. "Because you look half starved."

"Well, I'm not," Emily replied brusquely, once again infuriated by Daniel's assumption that she was weak and unable to care for herself, no matter how right he really was. She hated the way Daniel made her feel, like she was some kind of stupid child. "I was actually here to ask you about the electricity," she said. It was only a half-lie; she *did* need electricity at some point.

She wasn't sure but she thought she saw a flicker of disappointment in Daniel's eyes.

"I can get that fixed up for you tomorrow," he said, in a dismissive kind of tone, one that told her he wanted her off his doorstep and out of his hair.

Emily felt suddenly very awkward, and concerned that she'd said something to anger him. "Look, why don't you come over for some tea?" she said hesitantly. "As a thank-you for the shoveling and the oil delivery. And to apologize for earlier." She smiled hopefully.

But Daniel wasn't budging. He folded his arms and raised an eyebrow. "You expect me to want to hang out at your place? What, because your house is bigger so you think everyone wants to be there?"

Emily grimaced, confusion bubbling inside of her. She didn't know what she'd said to warrant Daniel's response, but she wasn't prepared to get into another vexing conversation with him. "Forget it," she mumbled.

She turned on her heel and stomped away, as annoyed with herself and her behavior as she was with Daniel.

But just a few moments later as she slumped beside the fireplace, her stomach growling with hunger, she heard a scratching sound coming from the front door. It was instantly familiar to her— the same sound that she'd heard last night—and she knew that meant Daniel had left another gift for her.

She raced to the door, heart pounding, and flung it open. Daniel had already disappeared. Emily looked down and saw on the doorstep was a thermos flask. She picked it up, unscrewed the lid, and sniffed. Immediately she smelled the same delicious aroma that had been coming from Daniel's house. He had left some soup for her.

Unable to turn down the demands of her stomach, Emily grabbed the soup and began devouring it. It tasted amazing, like nothing she'd ever had before. Daniel must be an incredible cook, another skill to add to the plethora of them. A musician, avid reader, cook, and handyman—not to mention tasteful interior designer— Daniel's talents were really starting to stack up.

*

That night, Emily curled up in the master bed, more comfortable than she had been last night. She'd cleaned the covers and dusted every inch of the room, ridding the place of the smell of abandonment. It felt good to have the house in some kind of livable condition—even if some of the radiators were still not really working fully. But knowing she'd achieved something, had stood on her own two feet for the first time in seven years, really made her proud. If only Ben could see her now! She already felt so different from the woman she'd been when she was with him.

For the first time in a long time, Emily felt herself looking forward to the next day and what it would bring: specifically, electricity. If she had a working fridge and oven she could finally cook some food. Maybe even repay the favors that Daniel had been doing for her by making him a meal. She wanted to make things right with him before she left at the very least, since she had pretty much descended on his life and caused chaos.

The more Emily thought about the prospect of returning home, the more she realized she didn't want to. Despite the trials and tribulations she'd already experienced over the last two days in the house, she felt a sense of purpose here that she hadn't felt for years.

What exactly did she have back in New York worth returning for anyway? There was Amy, of course, but she had her own life and wasn't exactly available often. Emily thought then that maybe it would be a good idea to extend her vacation a little. A long weekend in the house was hardly enough to sort out anything, and it would be a waste of effort to get the electricity working if she was just going to pack up and leave again so soon after. A week would be a better amount of time. Then she'd really get to experience the house and Maine, really recharge her batteries and give herself some time to work out what it was she truly wanted.

Being in her parents' old room was cozy and comforting, and Emily was struck by a sudden memory of coming in here as a very young girl, snuggling up between them and listening to her father read her stories. It was something that became a habit, a way for her to be close to parents who seemed, to her young mind, preoccupied with her new baby sister, Charlotte. It was only through the lens of Emily's adult eyes that she realized it was less that they were preoccupied with Charlotte, and more that they were avoiding their doomed marriage.

Emily shook her head, not wanting to remember, not wanting to relive those memories she had spent so many years banishing. But no matter how hard she tried, she couldn't stop them flooding her mind. The room, the house, the little trinkets here and there that reminded her of her father, all of them were culminating in her mind, bringing back to her the terrible memories she'd tried so hard to forget.

39

Memories of how the stories in the large master bed had stopped abruptly one tragic day; the day Emily's life had changed forever, the day her parents' marriage had been dealt its final, undefeatable blow.

The day her sister died.

Chapter Five

After a night of deep, dream-filled sleep, Emily woke to the sensation of warmth on her skin. It was so unfamiliar to her now to not feel cold that she sat bolt upright, suddenly alert, and discovered a shard of bright sunlight streaming in through a gap in the curtains. She shielded her eyes as she pulled herself out of bed and went over to the window. Drawing back the curtain, Emily reveled in the sight that opened up before her. The sun was out, reflecting brilliantly off the snow, which was melting fast. On the branches of the trees beside her window, Emily saw water droplets trickling down from the icicles, the sunlight turning them into drops of rainbows. The sight made her breath catch. She had never seen anything so beautiful.

The snow had melted enough for Emily to decide it was possible to now venture into town. She was so hungry, as though Daniel's soup delivery the day before had reawakened the appetite she'd lost after the drama of breaking up with Ben and quitting her job. She dressed in jeans and a T-shirt, then put her suit jacket over the top because it was the only thing she had that even semi resembled a coat. She looked a little strange in the ensemble, but figured most people would be staring at the stranger with the beat-up car squatting in front of the abandoned house anyway, so her outfit was the least of her concerns.

Emily trotted down the steps into the hallway, then opened the front door to the world. Warmth kissed her skin and she smiled to herself, feeling a surge of happiness.

She followed the trench that Daniel had dug along the pathway and followed the road toward the ocean where she remembered the shops to be.

As she strolled along, it felt a little bit like she was walking back in time. The place was completely unchanged, the same stores that had been there twenty years previously still standing proud. The butcher shop, the bakery, it was all as she remembered. Time had changed them, but only in small ways—the signage was more garish, for example, and the products inside had modernized—but the feel was the same. She reveled in the quaintness of it all.

Emily was so wrapped up in the moment she didn't notice the patch of ice on the sidewalk ahead of her. She slipped in it and went sprawling on the ground.

Winded, Emily lay on her back and groaned. A face appeared above her, old and kindly.

"Would you like a hand up?" the gentleman said, extending his hand to her.

"Thanks," Emily replied, taking him up on his kind offer.

He pulled her back onto her feet. "Are you hurt?"

Emily cricked her neck. She was sore, but whether that was from falling off the sideboard in the pantry yesterday or slipping in the ice today it was impossible to tell. She wished she wasn't such a klutz.

"I'm fine," she replied.

The man nodded. "Now, let me get this right. You're the one staying up in the old house on West Street, aren't you?"

Emily felt embarrassment creep into her. It made her uncomfortable to be the center of attention, the source of small-town gossip. "Yes, that's right."

"Did you buy the house off of Roy Mitchell then?" he said.

Emily stopped short at the sound of her father's name. That the man standing before her knew him made her heart lurch with a strange sensation of grief and hope. She hesitated a moment, trying to collect her bearings, to piece herself back together.

"No, I, um, I'm his daughter," she finally stammered.

The man's eyes widened. "Then you must be Emily Jane," he said.

Emily Jane. The name was jarring to her. She hadn't been called that for years. It was her father's pet name for her, another thing that vacated her life suddenly on the day Charlotte passed away.

"I just go by Emily now," she replied.

"Well," the man said, looking her over, "aren't you all grown up?" He laughed in a kindly manner but Emily was feeling stiff, like her ability to feel had been sucked out of her, leaving a dark pit in her stomach.

"May I ask who you are?" she said. "How you know my father?"

The man chuckled again. He was friendly, one of those people who could put others at ease easily. Emily felt a little guilty about her stiffness, about the New York surliness she'd acquired over the years.

"I'm Derek Hansen, town mayor. Your father and I were close. We'd fish together, play cards. I came over for dinner at your house several times but I'm sure you were too young to remember."

He was right, Emily didn't remember.

"Well, it's a pleasure to meet you," she said, wanting suddenly to end the conversation. That the mayor had memories of her, memories that she didn't possess, made her feel strange.

"You too," the mayor replied. "And tell me, how is Roy?"

Emily tensed. So he didn't know her father had up and disappeared one day. They must have just assumed that he stopped coming to the house for his vacations. Why else would they have assumed otherwise? Even a good friend, like Derek Hansen claimed to be, wouldn't necessarily think that a person had disappeared into the ether never to be seen again. It wasn't the brain's first inclination. It certainly hadn't been hers.

Emily faltered, not knowing how to respond to the seemingly innocuous yet incredibly triggering question. She became aware that she was starting to perspire. The mayor was looking at her with a strange expression.

"He's passed on," she suddenly blurted, hoping it would cause an end to the questioning.

It did. His expression turned grave.

"I'm sorry to hear that," the mayor replied. "He was a great man."

"He was," Emily replied.

But in her mind, she was thinking: *was he?* He had abandoned her and her mother at the time they had needed him the most. The whole family was mourning the loss of Charlotte but it was only he who decided to run away from his life. Emily could understand the need to run away from one's feelings, but to abandon one's family she couldn't comprehend.

"I'd better get going," Emily said. "I have some shopping to do."

"Of course," the mayor replied. His tone was more sober now, and Emily felt responsible for having sucked the easy joy out of him. "Take care, Emily. I'm sure we'll run into one another again."

Emily nodded her goodbye and rushed away. Her encounter with the mayor had rattled her, awakening yet more thoughts and feelings she'd spent years burying. She hurried into the small general store and shut the door, blocking out the outside world.

She grabbed a basket and began filling it with supplies— batteries, toilet paper, shampoo, and a ton of canned soups—then went up to the counter where a rotund woman stood at the till.

"Hello," the woman said, smiling at Emily.

Emily was still feeling uneasy thanks to her encounter earlier. "Hi," she mumbled, barely able to meet the woman's eye.

As the woman began bleeping her items through and bagging them, she kept giving Emily the side eye. Emily knew instantly that it was because she recognized her, or knew who she was. The last thing Emily could deal with right now was another person asking about her father. She wasn't sure her fragile heart could handle it. But it was too late, the woman seemed compelled to say something. They were only four items into her overflowing basket. She was going to be stuck here for a while.

"You're Roy Mitchell's eldest daughter, aren't you?" the woman said, her eyes squinted.

"Yes," Emily replied in a small voice.

The woman clapped her hands excitedly. "I knew it! I'd recognize that mane of hair anywhere. You haven't changed a bit since I last saw you!"

Emily couldn't remember the woman, though she must have come in here often as a teenager to stock up on chewing gum and magazines. It was amazing to her how well she had disengaged herself from the past, how well she had erased her old self to become someone else.

"I have a few more wrinkles now," Emily replied, trying to make polite conversation but failing miserably.

"Hardly!" the woman cried. "You're as pretty as you ever were. We haven't seen your family for years. How long has it been?"

"Twenty."

"Twenty years? Well, well, well. Time really does fly when you're having fun!"

She bleeped another item through the till. Emily silently willed her to hurry up. But instead of placing the item in the bag, she paused, the carton of milk hovering over the bag. Emily looked up to see the woman staring into the distance with a faraway look in her eyes and a smile on her face. Emily knew what was coming: an anecdote.

"I remember when," the woman began and Emily braced herself, "your father was building a new bike for your fifth birthday. He was scouring for parts all over town, haggling for the best deal. He could charm anyone, couldn't he? And he did love his yard sales."

She was beaming at Emily now, nodding in a way that seemed to suggest she was encouraging Emily to remember too. But Emily couldn't. Her mind was blank, the bike nothing more than a phantom in her mind conjured by the words the woman spoke.

"If I recall," the woman continued, tapping her chin, "he ended up getting the whole thing done, bell, ribbons, and all, for less than ten dollars. He spent the whole summer making it up, burned himself to a crisp in the sunshine." She started to chuckle, and her eyes were sparkling with the memory. "Then we'd see you whizzing round town. You were so proud of it, telling everyone daddy had made it for you."

Emily's insides were a roiling, molten pit of volcanic emotion. How could she have erased all of these beautiful memories? How had she failed to cherish them, these precious days of carefree childhood, of familial bliss? And how had her father walked away from them? At what point had he gone from being the kind of man who would spend all summer building a bike for his daughter to the kind of man who walked out on her never to be seen again?

"I don't remember it," Emily said, her tone coming out brusquely.

"No?" the woman said. Her smile was starting to fade as though cracking at the seams. It now looked like it was plastered there out of politeness rather than naturally there.

"Could you…" Emily said, nodding at the can of corn in the woman's paused hand, trying to prompt her to continue.

The woman looked down, almost startled as though she'd forgotten why she was there, as though she'd thought she were chatting with an old acquaintance rather than serving her.

"Yes, of course," she said, her smile disappearing entirely now.

Emily couldn't cope with the feelings inside her. Being in the house had made her feel happy and content, but the rest of this town made her feel horrible. There were too many memories, too many people sticking their noses in her business. She wanted to get back to the house as quickly as possible.

"So," the woman said, not willing or able to stop her inane chatter, "how long are you planning on staying?"

Emily couldn't help but read between the lines. The woman meant, how long will you be intruding on our town with your surly face and snappy demeanor?

"I'm not sure," Emily replied. "Originally it was a long weekend but I'm thinking maybe a week now. Two, possibly."

"Must be nice," the woman said, bagging up Emily's final item, "to have the luxury of a two-week break whenever you want it."

Emily tensed. The woman had gone from pleasant and happy to downright rude.

"How much do I owe you?" she said, ignoring the woman's statement.

Emily paid up and grabbed her bags to her chest, rushing out of the shop as quickly as she could. She didn't want to be in town anymore, it was making her feel claustrophobic. She rushed home, wondering what it was exactly that made her father love this place so much.

*

Emily arrived home to discover that an electric truck was parked outside. She quickly put her experience in town behind her, pushing away the negative emotions she was feeling just as she'd learned to do as a child, and allowed herself to feel excited and hopeful about the prospect of having sorted out another major issue with the house.

The truck rumbled to life and Emily realized they were just about to leave. Daniel must have let them into the house on her behalf. She set her bags down and jogged after them, waving her arms as they pulled off from the curb. Spotting her, the driver stopped and cranked down the window, leaning out.

"Are you the homeowner?" he said.

"No. Well, sort of. I'm staying there," she said, panting. "Did you manage to get the electricity on?"

"Yeah," the man said. "Stove, fridge, lights, we checked them all and everything works now."

"That's great!" Emily said, ecstatic.

"Thing is," the man continued, "you've got some surge issues going on. Probably because the house is in such disrepair. You might have mice in there chewing on the cables, something like that. When was the last time you were up in the attic?"

Emily shrugged, her excitement starting to wane.

"Well, you might want to get a service man out to look around up there. The electric system you have is outdated. Kind of a miracle we got it on to be honest."

"Okay," Emily said in a weak voice. "Thanks for letting me know."

The electric man nodded. "Good luck," he said, before driving away.

He hadn't said it, but Emily could hear the rest of his sentence in her head: *you're going to need it.*

Chapter Six

Emily woke late on the third day. It was almost as if her body could tell it was Monday morning and that she would usually be rushing to work, shoving past commuters to get onto the metro, squeezing in beside bored, half asleep teenagers chewing gum and businessmen with their elbows protruding as they refused to fold up their papers, and had decided to let her have a well-earned lie-in. As she peeled off the covers, groggy-headed and bleary-eyed, she wondered when the last time had been that she'd slept in past 7 a.m. She probably hadn't done so since her twenties, since before she met Ben, a time when hitting the town with Amy had been her modus operandi.

Down in the kitchen, Emily spent a long time brewing coffee in a coffee pot and cooking up pancakes using the ingredients she'd bought from the local store. It filled her heart with pleasure to see the now overflowing cupboards, to hear the buzz of the fridge. For the first time since leaving New York, she felt like she'd gotten herself together, at least enough to survive the winter.

She savored every bite of her pancakes, every sip of her coffee, feeling well-rested, warm, and rejuvenated. Instead of the sounds of New York City, all Emily could hear were the distant lapping waves of the ocean and a gentle, rhythmic dripping sound as more icicles melted. She felt at peace for the first time in a long time.

After her relaxing breakfast, Emily cleaned the kitchen from top to bottom. She wiped all the tiles, revealing the intricate William Morris design beneath the grime, then buffed the glass in the cupboard doors, making the stained-glass motifs sparkle.

Empowered by having gotten the kitchen into such great shape, Emily decided to tackle another room, one she hadn't even looked in yet for fear its decayed state would upset her. And that was the library.

The library had been by far her favorite room as a child. She loved the way it was divided in half by white wooden pocket doors so that she could shut herself into a reading nook. And of course she loved all the books it contained. Emily's dad hadn't been a snob when it came to books. His thinking was that any written text was worth reading, and so he had allowed her to fill the shelves with teenage romance novels and high school dramas, with tacky front covers depicting sunsets and silhouettes of hunky males. It made Emily laugh as she wiped the dust off their jackets. It was like an

48

awkward piece of her history had been preserved. Had the house not been abandoned for so long, she surely would have thrown them out at some point in the intervening years. But because of circumstance they had remained, gathering dust as the years passed by.

She placed the book in her hands back on the shelf as a sense of melancholy settled over her.

Next Emily decided to heed the advice of the electrician and go up into the attic to check the wiring. If they were indeed damaged by mice she wasn't sure what her next move would be—spend the necessary money on repairs or just tough out the rest of her time in the house. It didn't seem sensible to invest in the property if she was only going to be there for a fortnight at the most.

She pulled down the retractable ladder, coughing as a cloud of dust cascaded from the darkness above her, then peered up through the rectangular space that had opened up. The attic didn't freak her out as much as the basement did, but the thought of spider webs and mildew didn't exactly fill her with enthusiasm. Not to mention the suspected mice…

Emily climbed the stairs carefully, taking each one slowly, ascending into the hole an inch at a time. The higher she went, the more of the attic she could take in. It was, as she suspected, filled to the brim with items. Her dad's trips to yard sales and antiques fairs often yielded more items than could be feasibly displayed in the house, and her mom had banished some of the more unsightly ones to the attic. Emily saw a dark wooden tallboy which looked like it could have been a good two hundred years old, a sewing stool in faded green leather, and a coffee table made of oak, iron, and glass. She chuckled to herself, imagining her mom's face when Dad had hauled all this stuff home. It was so far from her taste! Her mom liked things modern, sleek, and clean.

No wonder they were going to divorce, Emily thought wryly to herself. If they couldn't even agree on interior design, what hope did they have agreeing on anything else!

Emily emerged fully into the attic and began looking around for any signs of mouse activity. But she found no telltale droppings or gnawed wiring. It almost seemed like a miracle that there weren't hordes of mice in the attic after so many years of abandonment. Perhaps they preferred the lived-in neighbors' homes, with their constant supplies of crumbs.

Content that there was nothing too concerning in the attic, Emily turned to leave. But her attention was piqued when she noticed an old wooden chest that stirred a memory, pulling it out from deep within her. She heaved the top of the chest open and gasped at the sight inside. Jewels; not real ones, but a collection of plastic beads and gemstones, pearls and cowries. Her dad had always made sure he brought back something "precious" for her and Charlotte and they would put them in the chest, calling it their treasure chest. It had become the centerpiece of every play they'd performed as kids, every make-believe game they'd engaged in.

Heart hammering from the vivid memory, Emily snapped the lid shut and stood quickly. She suddenly didn't feel like exploring anymore.

*

Emily spent the rest of the day tidying, careful to avoid any rooms that may trigger a melancholy mood. It seemed a shame to her if she spent the short amount of time she had here lingering on the past, and if that meant avoiding certain rooms in the house then she would do it. If she could spend her whole life avoiding certain memories, she could spend a few days avoiding certain rooms.

Emily had finally gotten around to charging her phone and had left it on the table by the front door—the only place she had any signal—in order to collect any texts she'd not received over the weekend. She was a little disappointed to see there were only two; one from her mom berating her for having left New York without telling her and one from Amy telling her to phone her mom because she'd been asking questions. Emily rolled her eyes and put her phone back, then went into the living room where she'd managed to get a fire going.

She settled down on the couch and flipped open the well-read teen romance she'd picked off the shelf in the library. It relaxed her to read, particularly when it wasn't anything that taxing. But this time she couldn't get into it. All the teenage relationship drama kept forcing her mind back to her own failed relationships. If only she'd realized as a kid when she'd first read these books that real life was nothing like that which was depicted in the pages.

Just then, Emily heard a knock coming from the front door. She knew immediately that it would be Daniel. There was no one else scheduled to come over, no carpenters, plasterers, or joiners, and certainly no pizza delivery. She hopped up and went into the hallway, then opened the door for him.

He stood there on the step, backlit by the porch light, moths dancing through the air around it.

"The electricity is working," he said, pointing at the light.

"Yup," she said, grinning, proud that she had achieved something he'd seemed so adamant that she could not.

"I guess that means you don't need me to deliver soup to your doorstep anymore," he said.

Emily couldn't tell from his tone whether he was making friendly banter or using the situation as another opportunity to berate her.

"Nope," she replied, her hand rising to the door as if readying herself to close it. "Was there anything else?"

Daniel seemed to be lingering, like there was something on his mind, words he didn't know how to speak. Emily narrowed her eyes, knowing, seemingly instinctively, that she was not going to like what she heard.

"Well?" she added.

Daniel rubbed the back of his neck. "Actually, yeah, I, um, ran into Karen today, from the general store. She, well, she didn't take too well to you."

"That's what you came to tell me?" Emily said, her frown deepening. "That Karen from the general store doesn't like me?"

"No," Daniel said defensively, "I was actually coming to find out when you were leaving."

"Oh well, that's a whole lot better, isn't it?" Emily bit back sarcastically. She couldn't believe what a jerk Daniel was being, coming over here and telling her no one liked her then asking when she would be leaving.

"That's not what I meant," Daniel said, sounding exasperated. "I need to know how long you're going to be here because it's up to me to keep this house in one piece over the winter. I have to drain the pipes, turn off the boiler, and do a host of things. I mean did you even consider how much it would cost you to heat this place over the winter?" Daniel regarded Emily's expression, which gave him all the answer he needed. "Didn't think so."

"I just hadn't thought about it yet," Emily replied, trying to excuse herself from his accusatory stares.

"Of course you hadn't," Daniel replied. "You just run through town for a few days, do some damage to this place, then leave me to pick up the pieces."

Emily was getting riled, and when someone challenged her or made her feel threatened or stupid, she couldn't help but feel the need to defend herself. "Yeah well," she said, her voice rising to a yelling volume, "maybe I'm not leaving in a few days. Maybe I'll stick around all winter."

She snapped her jaw shut, shocked to have heard the words come out of her mouth. She hadn't even had time to think them before she'd blurted them out, her mouth running away with her.

Daniel looked perturbed. "You'll never survive in this house," he stammered, just as shocked at the prospect of Emily sticking around in Sunset Harbor as she seemed to be. "It would eat you up. Unless you're rich. And you don't look rich."

Emily recoiled at the sneer on his face. She'd never been so insulted. "You don't know anything about me!" she cried, her emotions spilling over into genuine anger.

"You're right," Daniel replied. "Let's keep it that way."

He stormed away and Emily slammed the door shut. She stood there panting, reeling from the heated encounter. Who the hell was Daniel to tell her what she could or couldn't do with her life? She had every right to be in her father's home. In fact, she had more right than Daniel did! If anyone should be annoyed with the other's presence it should be her!

Fuming, Emily paced back and forth, making the floorboards creak and the dust swirl. She couldn't remember the last time she'd been so mad—even when she broke up with Ben and quit her job she hadn't felt the same hot lava pulsing through her veins. She stopped walking, wondering what it was about Daniel that riled her so much, that stirred angry passion within her in a way her partner of seven years had not been able to. For the first time since meeting Daniel, she wondered who he was, where he came from, what he was doing there.

And whether he had a significant other in his life.

*

Emily spent the rest of the evening ruminating on her latest argument with Daniel. As annoying as it was to be told the town folk didn't like her, and as frustrating as it was sharing her space with him, she couldn't help but admit she'd fallen in love with the old house. Not just the house, but the calm and quiet. Daniel had wanted to know when she was going home, but it was starting to dawn on her that this felt more like her home than anywhere else she'd lived in the last twenty years.

With a crackle of excitement running through her veins, Emily rushed to where her cell phone now stayed by the front door and dialed her bank. She went through the automated menu, punched in the necessary security codes, and listened to the robotic voice as it read aloud her balance. She jotted the figure down on a piece of paper balanced on her knee, the pen lid between her teeth, her phone wedged against her shoulder. Then she took the paper into the living room and began working out some sums: the cost of electricity and oil delivery, the fee and running costs of getting the Internet and a fixed landline installed, fuel for her car, food for the cupboards. Once she was done, she realized she had enough money to live off of for six months. She'd been working so hard for so long in a city that demanded it that she'd lost sight of the bigger picture. Now she had the opportunity to stop, to coast for a while. She'd be an idiot not to take it.

Emily sat back against the couch and smiled to herself. Six months. Could she really do it? Stay here, in her dad's old home? She was increasingly falling in love with the old ruin of a house, though whether that was because of it, the memories it stirred, or the connection she felt to her lost dad, she couldn't be certain.

But she resolved to fix it up, alone, and without Daniel's help.

*

Emily awoke Tuesday morning with a bounce in her step that she hadn't felt for years. Throwing open the curtains, she saw that the snow was now mostly gone, revealing the overgrown green grass of the grounds around the house.

Unlike her languorous breakfast of yesterday, Emily ate quickly and downed her coffee as quickly as a shot, before getting straight to work. The energy she'd felt while cleaning yesterday seemed to be a thousand times more powerful today, now that she knew she wasn't just staying here for a vacation but was setting up home for the next six months. Gone, too, was the claustrophobic sense of nostalgia she'd felt, the strong sensation that nothing should be touched, or moved, or changed. Before, she'd felt as though the house must be preserved, or restored to the way her father had wanted it. But now she felt like she was allowed to put her own stamp on it. The first step to achieving this was to sift through the mounds of possessions her father had amassed and sort the junk from the treasure. Junk, like her mounds of summer teen romances.

Emily rushed into the library, reasoning it was as good a place to start as any, and bundled the books up in her arms before taking them outside, strolling across the damp grass, and dumping them on the sidewalk. Across the road from the house was a rocky beach that sloped down to the ocean, barely a hundred yards away, and the distant, empty harbor.

It was still very cold outside—cold enough to turn her breath to coils—but there was a bright winter sun attempting to burst through the clouds. Emily shivered as she straightened up, then saw for the first time since she'd arrived that there was another person out on the sidewalk. It was a man with a brown beard and mustache, dragging a trash can behind him. It took Emily a little while to realize that he must live in the house next door—another Victorian-style mansion like her father's though in significantly better shape—and tried to re-categorize him in her mind as her neighbor. She paused, watching as he placed the can next to the mailbox then collected his mail—abandoned in the mailbox for days thanks to the snowstorm—before trotting across the well-kept grass and back up the steps of his enormous wooden porch. At some point, Emily would have to introduce herself. Then again, if she was as disliked as Daniel had suggested, maybe that wasn't so much of a priority.

As she walked back across her own lawn, Emily made a great effort not to look over at the carriage house, though she could smell the smoky scent of Daniel's wood burner and knew he was awake. She didn't need him coming over here, sticking his nose in her business, mocking her, so she went quickly back inside to search for more things that needed to be thrown out.

The kitchen was filled with junk—rusty utensils, colanders with broken handles, saucepans with burnt stuff at the bottom. Emily could see why her mom got so frustrated with her dad. He hadn't just been an antiques collector or bargain hunter, he'd been a hoarder. Perhaps her mom's love of the clean and sterile had been caused by her dad.

Emily filled a whole bin bag with bent spoons, chipped crockery, and various useless kitchen gadgets like egg timers. Then there were reams of baking paper, tin foil, kitchen roll, and all kinds of electronic equipment. Emily counted five blenders, six mechanical whisks, and four different types of weighing scales. She bundled them all up in her arms and carried them to the sidewalk, where she dumped them with the other bits of junk. It was starting to turn into a heap. The mustached man was out on his porch again, sitting in a deck-style chair, watching her, or, more specifically, watching the mound of junk that was slowly growing on the sidewalk. Emily got the sense he was less than thrilled by her behavior and so she waved in what she hoped looked like a friendly manner before retreating into the house to continue her purge.

At midday Emily heard the sound of a thrumming engine outside. She rushed out, excited to greet the service man who was coming to set up the phone line and Internet.

"Hi," she beamed from the door.

The day had brightened even more than she'd anticipated and she could see sunlight glinting off the ocean in the distance.

"Hello," the man replied, slamming the door to his truck. "My clients aren't usually so happy to see me."

Emily shrugged. As she led the man inside, she felt the eyes of the mustached man following her. *Let him stare*, she thought. Nothing was about to bring her mood down. She was proud of herself for having sorted out another necessity. Once the Internet was installed, she'd be able to order some things she needed. In fact, she'd order a whole shop online to avoid bumping into Karen again. If the townsfolk didn't like her, then she wasn't about to give them her business.

"Do you want tea?" she asked the Internet man. "Coffee?"

"That would be great," he replied as he bent down and opened his black tool bag. "Coffee, thanks."

Emily went into the kitchen and brewed up a fresh pot of coffee as the sounds of drilling emanated from the hallway. "I hope you take it black," she called out. "I don't have any cream."

"Black's fine!" the man shouted back.

Emily made a mental note to put cream on her shopping list, then poured two cups of steaming coffee, one for the service man and one for herself.

"You just moved into the place?" he asked as she handed him a cup.

"Sort of," she replied. "It was my father's house."

He didn't push her further, clearly inferring that she'd been left it in a will or something similar. "The electric system's pretty shoddy," he replied. "I'm guessing you don't get cable here or anything."

Emily laughed. If he'd seen the house just three days ago he wouldn't have needed to even ask the question. "Absolutely not," she replied jovially. Her dad had always loathed TV and had banned it from the house. He wanted his kids to enjoy the summer, not sit around watching TV while the world passed them by.

"Do you want me to hook you up?" the man said.

Emily paused, considering his question. She'd had cable TV back in New York. In fact, it had been one of her few pleasures in life. Ben had always derided her for her taste in TV, but Amy had shared the same love of reality shows and so she'd just talk to her about it. It became a sticking point, one of many, in their relationship. But he'd finally accepted that if he was going to spend every weekend watching sports she was allowed to watch the new season of *America's Next Top Model*.

Since coming to Maine, it hadn't even occurred to Emily that she'd missed all her favorite shows. And now, the idea of inviting that trash back into her life again seemed strange, like it would sully the house somehow.

"No, thanks," she replied, a little shocked to discover that her TV addiction had been cured just by getting out of New York.

"Okay, well, that's all done. Phone line's installed but you'll have to get a handset."

"Oh, I have a hundred," Emily replied, not exaggerating in the slightest—she'd found a whole box of them in the attic.

"Right," the guy replied, a little bemused. "The Internet's up and running too."

He showed her the Wi-Fi box and read out the password on the back aloud so she could connect her phone to the Internet. The moment she got her phone online, it, to her surprise, began vibrating, a constant stream of emails flooding in.

Her eyes glazed over as the counter in the corner kept going up and up and up. Amidst the spam emails and mailing list emails from her favorite clothing companies, there were a handful of sternly titled emails from her old company regarding the "termination" of her contract. Emily decided she'd read them later.

A part of her felt her privacy invaded by the Internet, the emails, and immediately longed for the past days when she had none. She was surprised to realize her own reaction, given how addicted she used to be to her email, her phone, hardly able to function without it. Now, to her shock, she actually resented it.

"Someone's popular," the service man said, chuckling as her phone vibrated again with another incoming email.

"Something like that," Emily mumbled, stowing her phone back in its perch by the front door. "Thank you, though," she added, turning to the service man as she opened the door. "I'm really glad to be connected to civilization again. It can get a little isolated out here."

"You're most welcome," he replied, stepping out onto the front steps. "Oh, and thanks for the coffee. That was really great. You should think about opening a cafe!"

Emily saw him out, mulling his words over in her mind. Maybe she *should* open a cafe. There wasn't one on the high street that she'd seen, whereas in New York there was one on every corner. She could just imagine the look on Karen's face if she decided to open her own store.

Emily got back to work cleaning the house, adding stuff to the mound on the sidewalk, scrubbing surfaces and sweeping floorboards. She spent an hour in the dining hall, dusting the picture frames and all the ornaments in the display cabinets. But just as she felt like she was finally getting somewhere with it all, she took down a hanging tapestry to shake the dust out and saw that behind it was a door.

Emily stopped short, staring at the door with a deep frown. She didn't have even the vaguest memory of the door, though she felt certain a secret door hidden beneath a tapestry would be the sort of thing she would have adored as a child. She tried the handle but found that it was jammed. So she rushed into the utility room and fetched a can of WD-40. After oiling the handle of the secret door, she was finally able to turn it. But the door itself felt like it was stuck fast. She rammed her shoulder against it once, twice, three times. On the fourth shove she felt something give, and with a final almighty push, she forced the door open.

Darkness opened up before her. She felt for a switch but couldn't find one. She could smell dust, the thickness of it getting in her lungs. The darkness and creepiness reminded her of the basement and she ran to get the lantern Daniel had left for her on the first day. As she brought the light into the darkness she gasped at the sight that opened up before her.

The room was enormous, and Emily wondered if it had once been a ballroom. Now, though, it was crammed with stuff, like it had been turned into yet another attic, yet another place to dump stuff. There was an old brass bedstead, a broken wardrobe, a cracked mirror, a grandfather clock, several coffee tables, a huge bookcase, a tall, ornamental lamp, benches, couches, desks. Thick cobwebs criss-crossed between all the items like threads tying everything together. Awestruck, Emily slowly paced around the room, the lantern light in her hands revealing mildewed wallpaper.

She tried to remember whether there was a time when this room had been used, or whether the door had been hidden beneath the tapestry when her dad had first purchased the house and he had never discovered the secret room. It didn't seem plausible to her that her dad wouldn't've known about this room, but she simply had no memory of it and so it had to have been closed off before she was born. If that was the case then this whole wing of the house had been abandoned longer than any other part, had been abandoned for an indeterminate amount of time.

It dawned on Emily that it would take even more effort to get the house cleaned out than she'd previously anticipated. She was exhausted from the day's work and still hadn't even made it to the upstairs yet. Of course, she could just shut the door and pretend the ballroom didn't exist, as her father clearly had, but the idea of returning it to its former majesty was too great a pull. She could picture it so clearly in her head; the floorboards buffed and gleaming, a chandelier hanging from the ceiling; she would be in a long silk dress, her hair up in a bouffant; and they would be twirling, waltzing together across the ballroom floor, she and the man of her dreams.

Emily looked at the heavy, massive objects in the room— couches, metal bed frames, mattresses—and she realized there was no way she'd be able to move them by herself, to fix up the ballroom alone. Getting the house in shape was a two-person job.

Though she'd resolved not to draw on his help, Emily had to admit for the first time that she needed Daniel.

*

Emily stomped out of the house, preemptively frustrated for the conversation she was about to have. She was a very prideful person and the idea of asking Daniel of all people for help irritated her.

She strolled across the backyard toward the carriage house. For the first time, the snow had melted enough to give her a clear look at the grounds and she realized how well kept they were, something that was clearly Daniel's doing. The hedges were all trimmed neatly and there were beds for flowers, bordered with neat pebbles. She could imagine it looking beautiful in the summer time.

Daniel seemed to have sensed her coming, because when she looked away from the hedgerow and back toward the carriage house, she saw that his door was open and he was standing with his shoulder wedged against the threshold. She could already read the look on his face. It said, "Come to grovel?"

"I need your help," she said, not even bothering to say hello.

58

"Oh?" was his only response.

"Yes," she said brusquely. "There's a room in the house I've discovered and it's full of furniture too big for me to lift. I'll pay you to come help move it all."

Daniel clearly didn't feel the need to respond right away. In fact, he didn't seem bound by the rules of normal social etiquette at all.

"I noticed you'd been doing some clearing out," he said at last. "How long are you planning on leaving that mound for? You know the neighbors will get twitchy."

"Leave the mound to me," Emily replied. "I just need to know if you'll come help out."

Daniel folded his arms, biding his time, making her stew. "How much work are we looking at?"

"To be honest," Emily said, "it's not just the ballroom. I want to clean out the whole house."

"That's ambitious," Daniel replied. "And pointless, considering you're only here for two weeks."

"Actually," Emily said, drawing the word out to delay the inevitable, "I'm staying for six months."

Emily felt a thick tension in the air. It was as though Daniel had forgotten how to breathe. She knew he wasn't particularly fond of her, but it seemed like rather an extreme reaction on his part, like someone had told him of a death. That her presence in his life could cause such palpable distress irked Emily immeasurably.

"Why?" Daniel said, a deep line creasing his forehead.

"Why?" Emily spat back. "Because it's my life and I have every right to live there."

Daniel frowned, suddenly confused. "No, I mean, why are you doing this? Going to all this effort to fix up the house?"

Emily didn't really have an answer, or at least not one that would satisfy Daniel. He just viewed her as a tourist, someone who breezed into town from the cities, made a mess, then swanned off back to their old lives. To think that she may *enjoy* a simpler life, that she may have a good reason for running away from the city, was clearly more than he could comprehend.

"Look," Emily said, growing irritable, "I said I'd pay you to help. It's just moving some furniture, maybe painting a bit. I'm only asking because it's more than I can do on my own. So are you in or out?"

He smiled.

"I'm in," Daniel replied. "But I'm not taking your money. I'm doing it for the sake of the house."

"Because you think I'll break it?" Emily replied, raising her eyebrow.

Daniel shook his head. "No. Because I love that house."

At least they had that in common, Emily thought wryly.

"But if I do this, know that this is strictly a working relationship," he said. "Strictly business. I'm not looking for any more friends."

She was stunned and irritated by his reply.

"Neither am I," she snapped. "Nor was I proposing it."

He smiled wider.

"Good," he said.

Daniel held out his hand for her to shake.

Emily frowned, uncertain about what she was getting herself into. Then she shook his hand.

"Strictly business," she agreed.

Chapter Seven

"The first thing we should do," Daniel said as he followed her down the path, "is get the plywood off the windows." He was holding his metal toolbox, swinging it as he walked.

"Actually, I really just want to get the old furniture out," Emily replied, frustrated that Daniel was already assuming the position of boss.

"You want to spend every day sitting in synthetic light when the sun's finally coming out?" Daniel asked. His question wasn't so much a question as a statement, though, and the subtext was that she was an idiot for wanting to do otherwise. His words reminded Emily a little of her dad, of the way he wanted her to enjoy the Maine sunshine rather than sit cooped up watching TV all day. As much as it pained her to admit it, Daniel did have a point.

"Fine," she said, relenting.

Emily remembered how her first attempt at removing the plywood had resulted in her smashing the window and nearly breaking her neck, and she was grudgingly relieved to have Daniel on board to help.

"Let's start in the living room," she said, trying to gain some control back over the situation. "It's where I spend most of my time."

"Sure."

There was nothing else to say, the conversation extinguished thoroughly by Daniel, and so they walked silently into the house, along the corridor, and into the living room. Daniel wasted no time setting the toolbox down and searching for his hammer.

"Hold the plank like this," he said, showing her how to support the weight of it. Once she was in position, he began popping the nails out with the clawed end of his hammer. "Wow, the nails are completely rusted."

Emily watched a nail fall to the floor and hit it with a thud. "Is this going to damage the floorboards?"

"Nope," Daniel replied, his focus completely on the task at hand. "But once we get some natural light in here it is going to show up how damaged the floorboards already are."

Emily groaned. She hadn't factored the cost of getting the floorboards sanded into her budget. Maybe she could rope Daniel into doing that as well?

Daniel popped the last nail and Emily felt the weight of the plywood drop against her body.

"Got it?" he asked, one hand still pushing the board against the sill, taking as much of the weight off her as possible.

"I've got it," she replied.

He let go and Emily staggered back. Whether it was her determination not to show herself up in front of Daniel again or something else, Emily managed not to drop the board, or whack it against anything, or generally make a fool of herself. She lowered it gently to the floor then stood up and clapped her hands.

The first shard of light burst in through the window and Emily gasped. The room looked beautiful in the sunlight. Daniel was right; sitting around in the electric light rather than the natural light would have been criminal. Starting with the windows was a great idea.

Enthused by their success, Emily and Daniel worked through the downstairs of the house, revealing window after window, letting the natural light fill the place. In most of the rooms the windows were massive floor to ceiling things, bespoke, clearly created especially for the house. In some place they were rotten or damaged by insects. Emily knew it would cost a lot to replace custom-made frames and tried not to think about it.

"Let's do the windows in the ballroom before we head upstairs," Emily said. The windows in the main part of the house were beautiful enough, but something told her the ones in the abandoned wing would be even better.

"There's a ballroom?" Daniel asked, as she showed him into the dining room.

"Uh-huh," she replied. "It's in here."

She drew the tapestry back, revealing the door behind, reveling in the look on Daniel's face. He was usually so stoic, so difficult to read, that she couldn't help but feel a small thrill at having caused him to experience shock. Then she opened the door and shone a flashlight inside the room, illuminating the vastness of it.

"Whoa," Daniel gasped, ducking his head so as not to hit the beam and gaping into the room. "I didn't even know this part of the house existed."

"I didn't either," Emily said, beaming, glad to share the secret with someone. "I can hardly believe it was hidden here all those years."

"It was never used at all?" Daniel asked.

She shook her head. "Not to my recollection. But someone used it once upon a time." She shone the light directly at the heap of furniture in the middle of the room. "As a dumping ground."

"What a waste," Daniel said. For the first time since Emily had met him, he seemed to be expressing genuine emotion. The sight of the hidden room was as mind-blowing to him as it had been to her.

They stepped inside and Emily watched as Daniel paced around in much the same way as she had when she'd first discovered the room.

"And you want to throw this all out?" Daniel said over his shoulder as he inspected the dust-covered items. "I bet some of this is antique. Expensive."

The irony of a room filled with antiques hidden in the house of an antiques enthusiast did not pass Emily by. She again wondered whether her dad knew about the room. Had he been the one to fill it with furniture? Or had it been like this when he bought the place? It just didn't make sense.

"I guess so," she replied. "But I wouldn't even know where to begin. I mean, you can see what I mean about there being some big pieces of furniture that I wouldn't be able to lift on my own. How would I go about selling it? Finding dealers?" That was her dad's world, a world she'd never really understood or had much enthusiasm for.

"Well," Daniel said, eyeing the grandfather clock. "You have Internet now, don't you? You could do some research. It would be a shame just to throw it all out."

Emily considered what he was saying, and was struck by one particular detail. "How did you know I had Internet?"

Daniel shrugged. "I saw the truck is all."

"I didn't realize you were paying such close attention to me," Emily replied with an air of faux-suspicion.

"Don't flatter yourself," came Daniel's dry response, but Emily noted that there was a wry smile on his lips. "We'd better get this stuff out of the way then," he added, breaking through her reverie.

"Yeah, great," she replied, snapping back to reality.

Daniel and Emily got to work removing the plywood from the windows. But unlike the windows in the main part of the house, when they got the plywood down and out of the way, the window that had been hidden beneath was made of beautiful Tiffany glass.

"Wow!" Emily cried, completely in awe as the room filled with different colors. "This is incredible!"

It was like stepping into a dreamland. The room was suddenly bathed in pinks, greens, and blues as the daylight rushed in through the window.

"I'm sure if my dad knew these windows were here he would have had this part of the house opened up," Emily added. "These are an antiquer's dream come true."

"They're pretty amazing," Daniel said, eyeing them in a practical way, admiring their intricate construction and the way the glass pieces fit together.

Emily felt like dancing. The light streaming through the window was so beautiful, so breathtaking, it made her feel carefree, as though she were made of air. If it looked this gorgeous in the winter sunshine, she couldn't begin to imagine how amazing this room would look once the bright summer sun was streaming through those windows.

"We should take a break," Emily said. They'd both been working for hours and this seemed a good a time to stop as any. "I could make us some food."

"Like a date?" Daniel said, shaking his head jokingly. "No offense, but you're not my type."

"Oh?" Emily said, joking along with him. "And what is your type?"

But Emily didn't get a chance to hear Daniel's response. Something had fluttered out from the ledge of the window, where it must have been lodged for years, and it had caught her attention. All the laughing and joking of a moment earlier disappeared, fading around her, as all her attention zoned in on the square piece of paper on the floor. A photograph.

Emily picked it up. Though it was aged, weathered, with mildew on the back, the photo itself wasn't particularly old. It was in color, though the colors had faded over time. A lump lodged in Emily's throat as she realized she was holding a photo of Charlotte.

"Emily? What's wrong?" Daniel was saying, but she could hardly hear him. Her breath had been stolen by the sudden sight of Charlotte's face, a face she hadn't seen for over twenty years. Unable to stop herself, Emily began to cry.

"It's my sister," she choked out.

Daniel peered over her shoulder at the photo in her trembling fingers.

"Here," he said, suddenly gentle. "Let me get that for you."

He reached out and took it from her grasp, then led her back out of the room, an arm around her shoulders. Emily let him guide her into the living room, too stunned to protest. The shock of seeing Charlotte's face had hypnotized her.

Emily, still crying, looked away from Daniel.

"I... I think maybe you should leave now."

"Okay," Daniel said. "As long as you're all right alone."

She stood up from the stool and gestured for Daniel to head toward the door. He watched her cautiously as though weighing whether it was safe to leave her in that state, but finally he collected up his tool box and headed for the door.

"If you need anything," he said on the threshold, "just call."

Unable to speak, she shut the door on Daniel then turned and pressed her back against it, feeling her breaths come in great shuddering gasps. She sank down to her knees, feeling darkness crowding in around her, wanting to curl up and die.

*

It was only the sudden shrill sound of her cell phone ringing that snapped her out of the horrible, suffocating sensation. Emily looked around, unsure how long she'd been curled up in a ball on the floor.

She looked up from her crumpled heap and saw her cell phone on the little table by the door blinking and vibrating. She stood up and saw, with surprise, Ben's name flashing up at her. She stared at the phone for a moment, watching it flash, watching his name fill the screen just as it had done a thousand times in the past. It was so normal, those three little letters, BEN, but suddenly so foreign, and so, so wrong in this house, at this moment, after seeing Charlotte's face, after being with Daniel all day.

Emily reached out and declined the call.

No sooner had the screen turned to black than it lit up again. This time it wasn't Ben's name, but Amy's.

Emily snatched the phone up, relieved for the lifeline.

"Amy," she gasped. "I'm so glad you called."

"You don't even know what I'm going to say," her friend quipped.

"I don't care. You could read the phone book for all I care. I'm just glad to hear your voice."

"Well," Amy said, "I do have something exciting to tell you actually."

"You do?"

"Yes. You know how we always used to talk about living in that converted church in the Lower East Side, and how awesome it would be?"

"Uh-huh," Emily said, not knowing where this was going.

"Well," Amy said, her tone sounding as though she were gearing up for a big reveal, "we totally can! The two-bed has just come on the rental market and we can totally afford it."

Emily paused, letting the information filter into her mind. When Amy and Emily had been students in New York, they'd constructed a whole fantasy about living in the converted church, surrounded by all the cool bars in the Lower East Side that they loved to frequent. But that had been back when they were in their twenties. That wasn't Emily's dream anymore. She'd moved on.

"But I'm happy here," Emily said. "I don't want to come back to New York."

There was a long pause on the other end of the phone. "You mean, ever?" Amy finally said.

"I mean for at least six months. Until my savings run out. Then I'll have to make other arrangements."

"What, like sleeping on my sofa again?" A hint of hostility had crept into Amy's tone.

"I'm sorry, Amy," Emily said, feeling deflated. "It's just not what I want anymore."

She heard her friend sigh. "You're really staying there?" she said finally. "In Maine? In a creepy old house? Alone?"

Emily realized then how strongly she felt about staying, how completely right it felt to her. And saying it aloud to Amy had made it completely real.

She took a deep breath, feeling confident and grounded for the first time in years. Then she stated simply, "Yes. I am."

3 months later

Chapter Eight

Spring sunshine seeped in through Emily's curtain, waking her as gently as a kiss. The slow, languorous mornings were something Emily enjoyed more and more as the days passed. She had grown to cherish the quiet stillness of Sunset Harbor.

Emily stirred in her bed and allowed her eyelids to flutter open. The bedroom that had once been her parents' was now very much her own. It had been the first room she'd restored and renovated. The old moth-eaten blanket was gone, replaced by a beautiful patchwork silk cover. The beautiful cream rug was soft and squishy beneath her feet as she got out of bed, using one post of the four-poster bed to pull herself to standing. The walls still smelled of fresh paint as she went over to the now sanded and varnished dresser and removed a floral spring dress. The drawers were neatly packed with clothes, her life once again organized.

Emily admired her reflection in the floor-length mirror, which she'd had restored and cleaned professionally, then pulled the curtains open fully, delighting in the way that spring had come to Sunset Harbor in a flurry of color; azaleas, magnolias, and daffodils bloomed in the yard, the trees bordering her property had grown lush green leaves, and the sliver of ocean she could see from the window was a glittering silver. She pushed open the window and breathed in deeply, tasting the salt in the air.

As she leaned out the window, she noticed movement in her peripheral vision. She craned her head to see better. It was Daniel, tending to one of the flower beds. He was completely focused on the task at hand, a habit Emily had come to recognize in him over the three months they'd been working on the house together. When Daniel started something, all his focus zoned in on it, and he wouldn't stop until it was done. It was a quality Emily respected in him, though at times she felt like she was completely pushed out. There had been plenty of times over the last few months when they had worked side by side all day and spoken not a single word. Emily couldn't work out what was going on in Daniel's mind; he was impossible to read. The only sign she had that he was not repulsed by her was that he came back day after day after day, following her requests to move furniture, sand floors, varnish wood, reupholster couches. He was still refusing to take any money, and Emily wondered how exactly he supported himself if he spent all his days with her working for free.

68

Emily drew back from the window and exited her bedroom. The upstairs corridor was now neat and organized. She'd removed the dusty picture frames from the wall and replaced them with a series of prints by the eccentric British photographer Eadweard Muybridge, whose photos were all about capturing movement. She chose the series of dancing women because to her they were incredibly beautiful, the moment of transience, the movement, it was like poetry to her eyes. The finger-smudged wallpaper had also been stripped and Emily had painted the hallway a crisp white.

Emily trotted downstairs, feeling more and more like this was her home. Those years she'd gate-crashed on Ben's life seemed to now be suddenly very far behind her. It felt to Emily that this was where she was always supposed to have been.

Her phone was in its usual spot on the table by the door. It felt like she'd finally gotten into a routine—waking up slowly, dressing, checking her phone. Now that spring had arrived, she had a new part to her routine, which was heading into town to grab coffee and breakfast before checking out the local flea markets for items that she wanted for the house. Today was Saturday, which meant there'd be more stores open for her to look in, and she was intent on finding more furniture today.

After firing off a text to Amy, Emily grabbed her car keys and went outside. As she crossed the yard she looked around for Daniel but could not see him. Over the last three months his presence had become another source of stability for her. It sometimes felt to Emily as though he was always there, just an arm's length away.

Emily got into her car—which she'd finally gotten repaired—and made the short drive into town, passing a white horse-drawn carriage on the way. Pony rides were one of Sunset Harbor's tourist activities—Emily could remember riding in the carriages as a child—and their presence indicated that the town was finally waking from its long winter hibernation. As she drove, she noticed a new diner had popped up on the high street. A little further down the road, the bar/comedy club was opening its doors for longer and longer hours. She had never seen a place transform so utterly before her eyes. The new hustle and bustle reminded her of her childhood summer vacations more so than at any point so far.

Emily parked up in a small parking lot beside the harbor. It was now quickly filling with boats, their masts bobbing up and down with the gentle tide. Emily watched the boats with a renewed sense of peace. It really felt to her like her life was just beginning. For the first time in a long time she saw a future for herself that she wanted:

living in the house, making it beautiful, being content and happy. But she knew it would not last forever. She only had enough money to sustain herself for three more months. Not wanting her dream life to end so soon, Emily had made the decision to sell off some of the antiques in the house. So far, she'd only parted with the ones that did not fit with her plans for the house and how it should look, but even selling those was agonizing for her, like she was giving away a part of her father.

Emily grabbed a coffee and bagel from the new diner, then ventured into Rico's indoor flea market. It was the same place her dad had visited every summer. Rico, its elderly owner, still owned the place. Emily was grateful that he hadn't recognized her the first Saturday she'd wandered in (due to his ailing eyesight and diminishing memory in equal parts) because it had given her the opportunity to introduce herself afresh, to get to know him on her own terms rather than with the shadow of her father's presence looming over her.

"Good morning, Rico," she called as she ducked into the dark shop.

"Who's that?" a disembodied voice called from somewhere in the darkness.

"It's Emily."

"Ah Emily, welcome back."

Emily knew he just pretended to remember her every time she came into the store, that his memory between each of her visits faded, and she couldn't help noting the irony that the person who liked her the most in Sunset Harbor only did so because he couldn't fully remember who she was.

"Yup, from the big house on West Street, just here to pick up that set of dining chairs," she called back, glancing around her, looking for the man.

Finally, he popped up from behind the counter. "Of course, yes, I've got it written down here." He placed his glasses on his thin nose and squinted through them at the book on the desk, searching for the scrawling handwriting that told him she was indeed Emily and that he had indeed sold her six dining chairs. Emily had learned after her first trip to the store (whereby she'd reserved a large rug only to discover it gone when she went to pick it up) that if Rico didn't write something down it as good as didn't happen.

"Righteo," he added. "Six dining chairs. Emily. Nine a.m. Saturday twelfth. That's today, isn't it?"

"That's today," she replied with a smile. "I'll just head out back and grab them, shall I?"

"Oh yes, oh yes, I trust you, Emily, you're a valued customer."

She grinned to herself as she went out back. She didn't know the designer of the chairs, only that the second she'd seen them she knew they were the perfect ones for the dining room. In some ways they looked like traditional chairs—wooden, four-legged, a back, a seat—but they'd been designed in a slightly quirky way, with the backs taller than the usual dining chair. They were painted sleek black, which would fit in perfectly with her new monochrome color scheme in that room. Seeing them again now excited her and she wanted to get them home ASAP so she could see them in place.

The chairs were heavy, but Emily had found that she'd become stronger over the last few months. All the physical labor required around the house had given her muscles she'd never achieved from working out at the gym.

"Great, thanks, Rico," she said as she began dragging the chairs toward the exit. "Will you be coming to my garage sale later today? I'm selling those two Eichholtz Rubinstein side tables, in need of a bit of TLC. Remember you said you might be interested in taking them and getting Serena to restore them?"

Serena was the spritely, boundlessly energetic young art student who drove two hours from the University of Maine every few weeks just to help out around the store fixing up furniture. She was always in jeans, her long dark hair swept over one shoulder, and Emily couldn't help but feel jealous of the calm, confident inner strength she possessed at such a young age. But because she was always friendly to Emily, despite the distrustful looks Emily had given her to begin with, Emily was now friendly with her.

"Yes, yes," Rico replied brightly, though Emily was certain he'd forgotten all about her garage sale. "Serena will pop along."

Emily watched as he jotted it down in his notebook. "The old house on West Street," she reminded him, just to make sure he didn't have to go through the embarrassment of asking her for her address. "I'll see you later!"

Emily loaded her trunk with the new chairs then drove back home through town, reveling in the sight of the spring flowers, the sparkling ocean, and the clear blue skies. When she pulled up to her house she was struck by how much it had changed. Not just from spring, which had brought color to the place and made the green grass on the lawn lush and thick, but from the sense that it was lived in, that it was once more loved. The plywood was all gone, the windows now clean and freshly painted.

Daniel had already made a good start on setting everything up on the lawn that she was planning on selling today. There were so many things that looked like junk to her but after Googling them it turned out that they were treasure to someone else. She'd cataloged all the items in the house that she didn't want to keep then checked the Internet to find out their true worth before posting on Craigslist what she was going to sell. She'd been shocked to receive a message from a woman in Montreal who was making the trip down solely to purchase a stack of TinTin books.

During those nights, while Emily had itemized the contents of the house, she'd started to understand what her father had seen in this strange pastime of his. The history of the pieces, the stories they carried with them, it all became so fascinating to Emily. The joy of discovering an antique amidst the junk was a thrill she'd never before experienced.

That wasn't to say there hadn't been a few disappointments along the way. An antique Grecian harp that Daniel had unearthed in the ballroom and that Emily had valued at $30,000 was, unfortunately, in such a state of disrepair that the specialist harp servicer said it would never be playable again. But he gave Emily the number of a local museum that took donations, and she was touched to discover that they'd affix a plaque to it to say it was donated by her father. It felt like a way of keeping his memory alive.

Looking at the yard filled Emily with a mixture of sadness and hope; she was sad to say goodbye to some of the items that her father had cluttered the house with, but she was also hopeful for the new house and how it would one day look. The future seemed suddenly bright.

"I'm back," she called out as she lugged the dining chairs into the house.

"In here!" Daniel replied, his voice carrying from the ballroom.

Emily set the chairs down in the hall and went in to find him. "You've made a great start getting that stuff out into the yard," she called out as she walked through the dining room and in through the secret door to the ballroom. "Anything I can help with?"

As she entered the ballroom, she stopped short, her voice stalling suddenly inside her throat. Daniel was wearing a white tank top and showing off muscles she'd only ever guessed at. It was the first time she'd gotten a real glimpse of his physique and the sight left her speechless.

"Yeah," he said, "you can grab the other end of this bookcase and help me carry it outside. Emily?" He looked at her and frowned.

She realized she was gaping and shut her mouth, then snapped back to attention. "Sure. Of course."

She went over to where he was standing, unable to sustain eye contact, and took her end of the bookcase.

But she couldn't stop her gaze from sliding over to his muscular arms as they strained from the weight of the bookcase as he straightened up.

Emily knew she was attracted to Daniel, accepted that she had been since the very first time they'd met, but he was as much of a mystery to her as ever. In fact, he was more of a mystery now because he'd spent so much time in her company without revealing much about himself at all. All she knew was that there was something in him that he kept hidden from view, some kind of darkness or trauma, some kind of secret he was running from that stopped him getting close. Emily herself knew how it felt to run away from a traumatic past life, so she never pushed it. And she had enough on her plate with unearthing the secrets of the house to even begin to work out how to unearth the secrets that Daniel held. So she left her attraction simmering beneath the surface, hoping it wouldn't boil over and set in course a chain reaction neither of them was prepared for.

*

The first customers began to arrive shortly after midday, as Daniel and Emily sat in deckchairs drinking homemade lemonade. Emily noticed Serena amongst them right away.

"Hey!" Serena called, waving, before bouncing over toward Emily and greeting her with a hug.

"You're here for those end tables, right?" Emily replied as they parted ways, Emily feeling a little uncomfortable at the physical intimacy Serena seemed so able to initiate. "They're just around the side this way, I'll get them for you."

Serena followed Emily through the maze of furniture set out on the lawn. "Is that your boyfriend?" she asked as they walked, looking back over at Daniel. "Because if you don't mind me saying, he is so hot."

73

Emily laughed and looked over her shoulder too. Daniel was speaking to Karen from the general store, still in his white tank top, the spring sun dancing across his biceps.

"He's not," she said.

"Not hot?" Serena cried. "Girl, are you blind?"

Emily shook her head and laughed. "I meant he's not my boyfriend," she corrected.

"But he *is* hot," Serena implored. "You know, you *can* say it out loud."

Emily smirked. Serena must think she was a complete prude.

They walked over to the two tables Serena had come to pick up. The younger woman crouched down to look them over, sweeping her dark hair over one shoulder, revealing the sun-kissed caramel-colored skin beneath. She was beautiful in that way unique to young women—with a glow and firmness that no amount of makeup could recreate.

"Are you thinking of making a move?" Serena asked, looking back up at Emily.

Emily almost choked on her breath. "Making a move on Daniel?"

"Why not?" Serena said. "'Cause if you don't, I will!"

Emily froze, suddenly feeling cold all over despite the spring sunshine. The thought of beautiful, carefree Serena with Daniel filled her with a jealousy so strong it took her by surprise. She could imagine that he would fall for her quickly, because how could he not? How could a man of thirty-five resist a young woman like Serena? It was practically written in their DNA.

Serena suddenly wiggled her eyebrows and flashed Emily a grin. "I'm just kidding! Wow, you looked like I'd told you someone had died!"

Emily couldn't help but feel a little irritated with Serena for pranking her. Pranks were just another thing the young and carefree could participate in. But for the jaded like herself, it was hard to enjoy.

"Why would you joke about that?" Emily asked, trying not to let her distress be audible.

"I wanted to see your face when I said it," Serena replied. "To see whether you were into him or not. Which you are, by the way, and you should totally do something about it. You know a guy who looks like *that* will not stay single for long."

Emily raised an eyebrow and shook her head. Serena was too young to understand how complicated things could be between two people, or know about the emotional baggage that weighed you down the older you got.

"Hey," Serena said, looking into the distance. "Have you had a chance to sort through the barn? I bet there's a ton of exciting things in there."

Emily looked behind her. Way across the lawn the wooden barn stood in the shadows, lonely and forgotten. She hadn't yet had a chance to explore the outbuildings. Daniel had told her about the greenhouses and how he'd wanted to restore them in order to grow flowers to sell but that it was too great a cost. The barn and other outbuildings, however, he had not mentioned, and she had simply forgotten about them.

"Not yet," she said, turning back to Serena. "But I'll let you know if I find anything you or Rico would like."

"Awesome," Serena said, backing up, an end tables in each arm. "Thanks for these. And don't forget to make a move on Mr. Hot Stuff. You're still young!"

Emily rolled her eyes and laughed to herself as she watched the younger woman swagger away. Had she been that confident in early twenties? If she ever had been she couldn't recall it. Amy had always been the confident one, Emily the shyer of the two. Perhaps that was why she always ended up in such terrible relationships, and why she'd stuck with Ben for so long; out of fear of not being able to find another person, of anguish about going through that awkward uncomfortableness of getting to know someone new.

Emily looked up at Daniel, watching the way he spoke to customers, the cautiousness in his mannerisms, and the way he became so quickly lost in his own world the moment he was alone again. For the first time since meeting him, Emily recognized something of herself in Daniel. And it was something that made her want to know him more.

*

Serena's interest in the barn had ignited a curiosity inside Emily. Later that evening, once the garage sale was done for the day, she ventured toward the outbuildings. In the fading light, the grounds of the house looked even more beautiful, and the care Daniel had taken over them became more apparent. He'd maintained a rose bush that had been growing on the grounds for as long as Emily could remember.

As she passed the broken greenhouse she had a flash of a memory, of bright red tomatoes growing in pots, of her mom in a floppy sun hat holding a gray watering can. There had been apple and pear trees behind the greenhouses. Maybe Emily would plant some again one day.

She passed the broken greenhouses and went up to the barn. The door was padlocked. Emily held the rusted padlock in her hand, trying to recall any memories of the barn. But she had none. Like the hidden ballroom, the barn was a secret she'd never thought to explore as a child.

She let go of the padlock—it fell back with a clunk—then went around the side to see if there was another way in. The small, grimy window was cracked but not big enough for her to get through. Then she noticed a patch-up job; one of the planks had clearly broken or succumbed to rot and a piece of flimsy plywood had been nailed over the top—a temporary measure that had never been revisited. Emily could picture her father out here, hammer in hand, covering the hole with a piece of plywood, thinking he would be back to do a proper job the next day. Only he never did. Shortly after fixing the damage to the barn, he'd decided to leave and never return.

Emily sighed deeply, frustrated with the intrusion of an imagined memory. She had enough real anguish to deal with; she couldn't cope with fake pain as well.

With a small amount of maneuvering, Emily was able to pry the plywood away, revealing a larger hole than expected. She got through it easily and found herself standing in the dark barn. There was a strange musty smell in the air that Emily couldn't place. What she could work out, however, was what was around her. The barn had been converted into a makeshift darkroom, somewhere where photographs could be developed. She tried to remember whether this was a hobby her father had had, but her mind came up blank. He had enjoyed taking photos of the family, that much she could remember, but never to the extent that he'd want to set up an entire darkroom for the purpose.

Emily walked over to the large, long table where different trays sat side by side. She'd seen enough movies to know that this was where the developing fluids would be poured. Then there was a clothesline strung across the table with pegs still on them from when the photos would be hung up to dry. The whole thing seemed very curious to Emily.

She wandered around the barn a little more to see if there was anything else of interest within it. At first, there was very little of note. Just bottles of developing fluid, old canisters for film reels, long lenses, and broken cameras. Then she found a door, which was also padlocked. Emily wondered where it led to and what was behind it. She looked around for a key but could find none. In her search, she discovered a box filled with photo albums, all stacked up haphazardly one on top of the other. She took out the first one, blew the dust from the cover, and opened it up.

The first image was black-and-white, an extreme close-up of a clock face. The next, also black-and-white, showed a broken window and a cobweb strung across it. Emily turned each page, frowning at the images. They didn't look professional to her, more like they were taken by an inexperienced hand, but there was a melancholy feel to them that seemed to reveal the mood of the photographer. In fact, as she studied each photo, she felt more as though she were looking into the mind of the photographer rather than analyzing the subjects he'd chosen to capture. The pictures made her feel almost claustrophobic, even though she was in a large barn, and deeply sad.

Suddenly there was a noise behind Emily. She swirled round, heart hammering, and dropped the photo album at her feet. There, standing in the gap through which she'd also entered the barn, was a small terrier. He was clearly a stray, his fur matted and unkempt, and he stood there staring at her, bemused that someone was standing in his patch.

That explains the smell, Emily thought.

She wondered whether Daniel knew about the stray dog, had seen him wandering around the grounds at all. She decided she'd ask him about it tomorrow when the garage sale continued—as well as about the discovery of the darkroom—and found herself excited to know she'd have a reason to talk to him.

"It's okay," she said aloud to the dog. "I'm just leaving."

It tipped its head to the side as though listening to her words. She scooped up the photo album to place it back in the box, then saw that one of the pictures had fallen out from between the pages. She picked it up and saw that it was a photo of a birthday party. Young children were seated around a table and there was a huge pink cake made to look like a castle in the middle. Suddenly, Emily realized what she was looking at—it was a picture of Charlotte's birthday. Charlotte's fifth birthday. Charlotte's last birthday.

Emily felt the tears prick her eyes. She held the picture tightly in her trembling hands. She had no real memories of Charlotte's last birthday, just like she had few memories of Charlotte herself. It was as though her life had been cleaved in two—the first part was life when Charlotte was alive, the second part was life after her death, the part where everyone broke down, where her parents' marriage finally fell apart after the strain of their silences became too much, and the grand finale whereby her father disappeared off the face of the earth. But that had all happened to Emily Jane, not to Emily, not to the woman she'd decided to become, the person she'd cleaved out of the wreckage. Looking at the photo here, at the evidence of life with Charlotte, Emily felt closer to the child she'd left behind than ever before.

The dog barked, and Emily's gaze snapped up. "Okay," she said, "I get it. I'm leaving."

Instead of returning the photo album to the box, Emily grabbed the whole thing, noting as she did so that the box beneath it was also packed with photographs, then trudged through the barn before squeezing back out of the hole. Her mind was exploding with thoughts. The hidden ballroom, the secret darkroom, the locked door in the barn, the box full of photographs… what other secrets was this old house hiding?

Chapter Nine

As she raced back into the house, her arms laden with photo albums, Emily was acutely aware of the sounds of hammering and drilling coming from the ballroom. That meant that despite the late hour, Daniel was still inside hanging picture frames and mirrors for her. He'd been working later and later into the evening, sometimes as late as midnight, and Emily had begun to entertain the thought that he was doing it to be close to her, to maintain a sense of proximity, as if he waited for the moment she brought in a cup of tea for him as keenly as she did. It was often around this time of the evening, after she was done organizing and rummaging for the day, that she'd pop her head around the door and catch up with him. He would be expecting her to do so tonight as well.

But tonight her mind was elsewhere. In fact, seeing Daniel was the last thing she wanted to do. She'd been so shaken up by the photograph of Charlotte, by the discovery of the darkroom, that she'd become solely focused on what she wanted to do next, what she *needed* to do, right now. At last.

Because there were still rooms within the house that Emily hadn't been in yet—rooms she had very deliberately avoided entering. One was her father's study, and it was here that she was heading. Even after months of living in the house, the door to his study had been kept tightly shut. She hadn't wanted to disturb it. Or, more likely, she hadn't wanted to let out whatever secrets it held.

But now she felt like too much had remained hidden for too long. The mysteries in her family were eating her up. She'd let the silences, the not knowings, take over her mind. No one in her family had ever spoken about anything—of Charlotte's death, of her mom's subsequent breakdown, of her parents' impending divorce which advanced closer with every year that passed. They were cowards—letting their wounds fester rather than taking action. Her mom, her dad, they were both the same, leaving so much unspoken, letting the wounds became gangrenous until the only course of action was to sever the limb.

Sever the limb, Emily thought.

That was exactly what her father had done, wasn't it? He'd severed his entire family, had run away from whatever problem it was he was unable to speak about. He'd walked out on all of them because of some obstacle, some hurdle, that he deemed insurmountable. Emily didn't want to spend her whole life

79

wondering. She wanted answers. And she knew she would find them in that study.

She dumped the box of photos on the stairs before climbing them two at a time. Her mind raced frantically as she strode with purpose along the upstairs corridor until she reached the door of her father's study and paused. The door was made of dark varnished wood. Emily remembered staring up at it as a youngster. It had seemed imposing back then, almost menacing, a door through which her father would disappear as though swallowed up, only to emerge hours later. She was never allowed to disturb him and, despite her curiosity as a child, she'd never broken the rules and gone inside. She didn't know why she wasn't allowed in. She didn't know why her father would disappear inside. Her mom told her nothing, and as the years passed and she grew into a teenager, she'd adopted a couldn't-care-less attitude about the room, wrapping her unanswered questions in a blanket of silence.

She tried the doorknob now and was surprised to discover that it turned. She'd assumed the study would be locked, that it would put up some kind of resistance to her intrusion. So it came as a shock to her to realize she could just walk straight into a room she'd never set foot inside before.

She hesitated, almost as if waiting for her mother to appear and scold her. But of course no one came, so Emily took a deep breath and pushed open the door. It swung open with a creak.

Emily peered into a room of shadows. Inside she saw a large desk, filing cabinets, and bookshelves. Unlike the rest of the house, her dad's study was tidy. He hadn't filled it with objects or artwork or photographs; there were no mismatched rugs overlaid on the floor because he couldn't decide which one to buy. In fact, of every room in the house she'd been in, this one was the least like her father's. The incongruity was disconcerting.

Emily paced inside. There was the familiar smell of dust and mildew in the air, the same smell that had permeated the whole house when she arrived. Cobwebs hung from the ceiling, in between the lightbulb and its shade. She inched past them, not wanting to disturb any lurking creepy crawlies.

Once fully inside, Emily wasn't really sure where to begin. In fact, she didn't even know what it was exactly that she was looking for. She just had a feeling that she would know as soon as she saw it, that the mysteries of her family were hidden somewhere in this room.

She went over to the filing cabinet and began rummaging through the first drawer, deeming it as good a place to start as any. Amongst her father's papers she found legal deeds to the house, her parents' marriage certificate, and divorce proceedings from her mom. She found a prescription slip for Zoloft, an antidepressant. It didn't really surprise her to know her father was medicated—the death of a child could send anyone into a spiraling depression. None of it helped explain her father's disappearance.

Once she'd searched through the filing cabinet and examined the papers inside, Emily moved over to the desk to look in the drawers there. The first one she tried to open was locked, and Emily muttered a small *a-ha* under her breath. She was about to call Daniel up to see if he could jimmy the lock and get the drawer open for her, when her attention fell to a small vault in the corner of the room. At once Emily was hit by the distinct feeling that whatever was inside that vault would answer every burning question in her mind.

She abandoned the drawer and raced over to the vault, kneeling down beside the dark green steel reinforced safe. She saw that it was fastened with a padlock that required a combination rather than a key. With trembling fingers, Emily twisted the little silver dials around, trying her dad's birthday first. But the combination wasn't right and the padlock didn't budge. Then a little voice in her mind told her that Charlotte's birthday would surely be the combination needed to open the lock. Charlotte had been her dad's favorite child, after all. But when she entered the numbers, she found that that didn't work either. As a last stab, Emily clicked the numbers around until her own birthday was staring up at her. When she pressed on the padlock, she was surprised to discover that it popped open.

Emily sat back, stunned. She had always blamed herself for her father leaving (like every child inevitably does when a parent walks out of their life), because she thought that she wasn't enough like Charlotte, that Charlotte had been her dad's favorite child and losing her had been his first grief, his second being that Emily was not a good enough substitute. And those pictures she'd found of Charlotte in the house, the way they'd literally fallen out of the woodwork as though they were sewn into the fabric of it, had just confirmed that long-held belief. But Emily was now being suddenly confronted with a new reality. *Her* birthday was the combination to access the vault. Her dad had specifically chosen it. Because whatever was inside was for her eyes only? Or because her dad had loved her just as fiercely as he'd loved Charlotte?

Emily's hand shook as she reached out and removed the padlock from the vault's door. Then she pulled on the door. It squealed open.

Emily reached her hand into the unknown, feeling around. She felt some kind of fabric, velour or velvet, and pulled it out. She looked down and saw in her hand she was holding a dark red pouch with a darker red ribbon. It was heavy and Emily frowned. She unfastened the ribbon and tipped the pouch up. A stream of pearls fell into her hand, connected by a thin white thread. Emily recognized the necklace immediately. Many years ago, when she and Charlotte were performing one of their pirate plays for their parents, she'd been playing the part of a kidnapped princess. She'd worn the pearl necklace and her father, upon seeing it, had become very angry and demanded she remove it. Emily had cried, her mom had shouted at her dad for his overreaction, and the necklace had disappeared never to be seen again.

It was several days later before he'd calmed down enough to explain to her that the necklace had belonged to his mother. It was several years later that she understood why it held such important sentimental value to him; it was the only item his mother hadn't been forced to pawn to pay for his education. They never spoke of the necklace again and Emily hadn't seen it, though she'd thought of it often.

Now Emily stared at the necklace in her hand, feeling a sense of disappointment. A pearl necklace didn't exactly answer her family secrets or explain the mystery of her father's disappearance. And it stung her to think that her father had felt that the only way to keep his most prized possession away from a curious, sticky-fingered five-year-old was by locking it up in a *vault* of all things. Unless the necklace was worth something and he'd hidden it here for safekeeping to make sure her mom couldn't pawn it off after he left? Because he was going to come back for it one day? Or because he wanted to make sure it found its way into Emily's possessions, as though it were a sort of apology to the five-year-old version of herself? What if he'd made the padlock code her birthday as a clue? There was no way of knowing for certain, without her dad here to explain it to her.

Emily played with the pearls with her fingertips. She felt like a brat for having been disappointed by them; if her dad had hidden them specifically for her she should be grateful. It was just that she'd been certain the vault would contain the information she so desperately needed. That the final piece of the puzzle would be inside.

She sighed and was about to shut the vault door back up when she noticed something else, hiding in the shadows, way in the back. She reached her hand inside and took hold of it. Pulling it out, she looked down into her palm and discovered that she was holding a keychain filled with keys.

Emily stared at the keychain in her hand, her heart hammering at the discovery. What could possibly have compelled her father to hide his keys in a vault? What secrets did he hold that were so bad he needed to lock the keys away?

There were at least twenty keys on the chain and Emily looked at each one in turn, wondering what doors they might open. Then she remembered the desk drawer, the one she'd found to be locked when she'd tried to look inside. She rushed over to the drawer and tried each key in the lock until one slid in. Then, suddenly, she heard a click.

That was it. She'd done it. She'd finally found whatever it was that her father had hidden so thoroughly and for so many years from the family.

She peered into the drawer. It contained one thing: a single white envelope. In neat handwriting that Emily instantly recognized as belonging to her father, one word was written in faded blue ink.

Emily.

A sensation like ice swept through Emily's body as she realized that her father had written a letter for her but never given it to her. That he'd hidden it away in a locked drawer, further locking the key in a vault. Emily had the distinct impression that whatever was inside that letter, it would change everything.

But before Emily even got the chance to open it, the doorbell suddenly rang. She jumped about a mile in the air and squealed. It was almost midnight. Who on earth would be calling at this hour?

*

Emily stuffed the letter into her pocket then leapt up and raced down the corridor. At the top of the stairs she saw that Daniel had beaten her to the door. It was standing open, and there on the step was a short, portly man wearing an outfit that looked like he'd just stepped off the golf course.

"Hey ho," he said to Daniel, his voice said floating up the staircase toward her. "Sorry for the late call. I'm Trevor Mann, your neighbor. I live in the hundred acres behind you and am just up for the season."

He held out a hand to Daniel. Daniel just stared at it. "This isn't my house," he said. "It's not my hand you need to shake."

Emily felt a small smile tug at her lips as Daniel turned and gestured to her standing at the top of the stairs. She bounded down and took hold of Mr. Mann's hand, shaking it firmly to make sure he knew who was boss.

"I'm Emily Mitchell. It's nice to meet you."

"Ah," Trevor said as friendly as ever. "Sorry for the mistake. Anyway, I won't keep you long, I know it's late. I just wanted you to know that I have my eye on your land and I'm hoping to take it over by the end of the summer."

Emily blinked, confused by his words. "I'm sorry, what?"

"Your land. I've had my eye on it for the last twenty years. I mean I know I already have a hundred acres while you have a mere five but you have the ocean view, which means you have one of the last prime lots on the water. It really would complete my lot to purchase it. This is your moment to cash in."

"I don't understand," Emily said.

"Don't you? Am I still speaking French?" He guffawed loudly as though he'd made the funniest joke in the world. "I want to buy your land, Miss Mitchell. You see, there's been all kinds of loopholes what with the owner being AWOL. But I noticed that there were lights on and asked around town. It was Karen in the general store who told me someone was occupying it again."

Emily and Daniel exchanged a brief bemused look.

"But it's not for sale," Emily said, her voice sounding stunned. "This is my father's place. I inherited it."

"Did you?" Trevor said, his tone still friendly in a way that didn't seem to match the words he was speaking. "Roy Mitchell isn't dead, is he?"

"Well, no, I don't know, he's..." Emily stuttered. "It's complicated."

"He's a missing person, as far as I understand it," Trevor said. "Which means the house is in a sort of legal limbo. Back taxes haven't been paid for years. There's all kinds of red tape around it." He chuckled. "I'm assuming by the blank look on your face you weren't aware of that."

Emily shook her head, confused and frustrated by Trevor's intrusion into her life, on this night of all nights, while the letter from her father burned in her back pocket. "Look, the land isn't for sale. This was my dad's house and I have every right to be here."

"Actually," Trevor said, "you don't. I forgot to tell you that I'm on the zoning board. Me and Karen and a whole bunch of other people who didn't take too kindly to you when you got here. I've taken it upon myself, as my neighborly duty, to inform you that due to the back taxes being unpaid, technically the town owns the house. Furthermore, it was declared uninhabitable years ago, so if you want to live here, you'll need a new certificate of occupancy. It is illegal to live here right now, do you understand?"

She scowled. At every step in her life, Emily had discovered, there had been people looking to keep her down, to tell her what she could *not* do—whether it was bosses, or boyfriends, or rude neighbors, they were all the same. All looking to be an authority on her head, to stop her from her dreams, to keep her down.

But she was done with authorities in her life.

"That may be so," she finally replied, "but that still doesn't make my father's house yours, does it?" She spoke with an equally steely grin, smiling wide, her expression, like his, not matching the hard venom in her voice.

His face finally fell—and his smile along with it.

"Our town can claim your house and auction it off," he insisted. "Then I can buy it."

"So why don't you?" she gambled.

His scowl deepened.

"Legally," he said, clearing his throat, "it would be far cleaner to buy it from you. That sort of legal situation could tie it up for years. And as I'd said, it's a gray area. Nothing like this has happened in our town before."

"A shame for you, then," she replied.

He stared back, tongue-tied, and Emily felt proud of herself for standing up to authority.

Trevor smiled an insipid smile. "I'll give you a little time to think about it. But really, I'm not sure what there is to think about. I mean, what will you do with this house? When the novelty wears off you will leave. Come back in the summers. Two months a year. Are you telling me you will live here year round? And do what? Be realistic. You will leave in the fall like all of them. Or run out of money." He shrugged and laughed again, as though he hadn't just threatened her and her livelihood. "The best thing for you to do is sell the land to me while the offer still stands. Why don't you make life easier on both of us and sell me your property?" he pressed.

"Before I call the police to evict you?" He looked at Daniel. "And your boyfriend," he added.

Daniel's eyes smoldered.

She held her ground.

"Why don't you get the hell off my land," she said, "and go back to your viewless hundred acres—before I call the police to convict you of trespassing?"

He looked like a deer in the headlights, and she had never been so proud of herself as at that moment.

Then he grinned, turned on his heel, and strolled away across the lawn.

Emily slammed the door shut so hard the whole house vibrated. She looked at Daniel, lost and bewildered, to find that the concern in his eyes matched her own.

Chapter Ten

Emily stood there, heart pounding, irate. Trevor Mann had really stirred her up.

But she could hardly reflect on her anger, his visit—because her mind was pulled back to the letter in her back pocket.

Her father's letter to her.

She reached in and pulled it out, examining it in awe.

"What a jerk," Daniel began. "Do you really think—"

But he stopped himself as he saw her expression.

"What have you got there?" Daniel asked frowning. "A letter?"

Emily looked down at the envelope in her hands. Plain. White. A standard size. It looked so innocuous. And yet she was so afraid of what it would contain. A confession to a crime? The revelation of a secret life as a spy, or as another woman's husband? What about a suicide note? She wasn't sure how she would cope if it were the last, and couldn't even begin to guess at her reaction if it was any of the former.

"It's from my dad," Emily said quietly, looking back up at him. "I found it locked away with his things."

"Oh," Daniel said. "Maybe I should go. I'm sorry, I didn't realize—"

But Emily reached out and put a hand on his arm so that he had to stay put. "Stay," she said. "Please? I don't want to read it alone."

Daniel nodded. "Shall we go and sit down?" His voice had become softer, more caring. He gestured toward the door to the living room.

"No," Emily said. "This way. Come with me."

She led Daniel up the stairs and down the long corridor which ended with her dad's study.

"I used to stare at this door when I was a kid," Emily said. "I was never allowed in. And look." She turned the handle and pushed the door open. With a little shrug she turned back to Daniel. "It wasn't even locked."

Daniel gave her a caring smile. He seemed to be treading on eggshells around her and she could fully understand why. Whatever was in the letter could be dynamite. It could set off some kind of catastrophic reaction in her brain, send her reeling, spiraling into despair.

They went inside the dark study and Emily sat down at her dad's desk.

"He wrote this letter right here," she said. "Opened this drawer. Popped it in. Locked it. Hid the key in that vault. And then walked about of my life forever."

Daniel pulled up a chair and sat beside her. "Are you ready?"

Emily nodded. Like a scared child peeping through their fingers during a scary movie, Emily could hardly look as she picked up the letter and tore open the top. She slid the paper from the envelope—it was just one piece of eight-by-eleven paper, folded in half. Her heart began to beat wildly as she opened it up.

Dear Emily Jane,

I don't know how much time will have passed between me leaving and you reading this letter. My only hope is that you haven't suffered for too long wondering about me.

That leaving you will be my biggest regret, I'm in no doubt. But I could not stay. I hope one day you'll accept why, even if you will never be able to forgive me.

I have only two things to tell you. The first, and you must believe me when I say this, nothing was your fault. Not what happened to Charlotte, nor the state of your mom's and my marriage.

The second is that I love you. From the first moment I saw you to the last. You and Charlotte were my greatest contributions to this world. If I never made that clear when I was around then I can only apologize, though sorry doesn't seem a big enough word.

I hope this letter finds you well, whenever it may be that you read it.

With all my love,

Dad

A million emotions swirling in her mind, Emily read and reread the letter, her grip on it tightening. Seeing her dad's words on the page, hearing his voice in her head speaking to her from twenty years in the past, made the absence of him seem even greater than ever.

She let the letter fall from her fingers. It fluttered to the tabletop, her tears falling after it. Daniel grabbed her hand as though imploring her to share with him, concern etched across his forehead, but Emily could hardly get the words out.

"For years I thought he left me because he didn't love me enough," she stammered. "Because I wasn't Charlotte."

"Who's Charlotte?" Daniel asked her kindly.

"My sister," Emily explained. "She died. I always thought he blamed me. But he didn't. It says so right there. He didn't think it was my fault. But that means if he didn't leave because he blamed me for her death then why did he leave at all?"

"I don't know," Daniel said, putting an arm around her and pulling her into him. "I don't think you can ever fully understand another person's intentions, or why they do the things they do."

"Sometimes I wonder if I even knew him at all," Emily said glumly into his chest. "All these secrets. All this mystery. The ballroom, the darkroom, for god's sake! I didn't even know he liked photography."

"Actually, that was me," Daniel said.

Emily paused, then moved out of the embrace. "What do you mean it was you?"

"The darkroom," Daniel repeated. "Your dad set it up for me years ago."

"He did?" Emily said, sniffing up her tears. "Why?"

Daniel sighed, shifted away. "When I was younger your dad caught me on the grounds. I was running away from home and knew you guys weren't here often. I figured I'd hide out in the barn and no one would notice me. But your dad found me. And instead of kicking my ass out, he gave me some food, a beer"—he looked up and grinned at the memory—"then asked me what I was running from. So I gave him the whole teenage spiel, you know. About how my parents didn't understand me. About how what I wanted for me and what they wanted for me were so different we could never find common ground. I was going off the rails in those days, flunking school, getting in trouble with the cops for dumb stuff. But he was calm. He spoke to me. No, he *listened* to me. No one else had done that. He wanted to know what I liked. I was embarrassed, you know, to tell him I liked taking photos. What sixteen-year-old boy wants to admit that? But he was so okay about all of it. And he said I could use the barn as a darkroom. So I did."

Emily thought of the photos she'd found in the barn, the black-and-white images that seemed to reveal the weariness of the soul that had taken them. She'd never imagined that the photographer was a kid, a young boy of sixteen struggling with his home life.

"Your dad urged me to go back home," Daniel added. "But when I refused, he made me a deal. If I finished school, he'd let me stay in the carriage house. So for that whole year I'd come up here. It became my sanctuary. Thanks to him I finished school. I was looking forward to seeing him again, to tell him. I idolized him, wanted to show him what I'd done and how much he'd helped me, how I'd straightened myself out because of him." Daniel looked at her then, making eye contact so intense she felt electricity crackle in her veins. "He didn't come back that summer. Or the next summer. Or ever again."

The impact of his words hit Emily forcefully. That her father's disappearance could have affected someone other than herself had not occurred to her, but here was Daniel, baring his soul, sharing the same pain she did. The not knowing what had happened, the empty space it created inside, Daniel knew what that felt like too.

"That's why you help out on the grounds?" Emily said, quietly.

Daniel nodded. "Your dad gave me a second chance in life. Only one who ever had. That's why I keep this place up."

They both fell silent. Then Emily looked up at him. Of all the people in the world, Daniel seemed to be the only one as affected by her father's disappearance as she was. They shared this. And something about that bond made her feel close to him in a way she never had before.

Daniel's eyes roved over her face, seeming to read her mind. Then he brought his hands up to her jaw and cupped her cheek. He drew her into him slowly and she breathed in the scent of him—the pine trees and fresh grass, smoke from the wood burner.

Emily's eyes fluttered closed and she leaned into him, anticipating the feel of his lips on hers. But nothing happened.

She opened her eyes at the same time as Daniel's encircled arms loosened.

"What's wrong?" Emily said.

Daniel exhaled loudly. "My mom wasn't a great woman but she gave me one piece of great advice. Never kiss a girl when she's crying."

And with that he stood up and began to walk slowly across the study to the door. Emily felt herself deflate. She shut the door softly behind him and then leaned against the door and slid down to the floor, letting her tears fall once more.

Chapter Eleven

The next morning, Emily hadn't even had time to change out of her pajamas when she heard the doorbell ring. As she hurried down the stairs she thought about last night. She'd slept terribly, having cried herself to sleep. Now she felt muggy-headed and more than a little embarrassed that she'd subjected Daniel to that outpouring of emotion, that she'd dragged him down with her. And then there was the kiss that never happened. She wasn't even sure she'd be able to look him in the eye.

She got to the door and pulled it open.

"You're early," she said, smiling, trying to act normal.

"Yeah," Daniel said, shifting from one foot to the other. His hands were deep in his pockets. "I thought maybe we could have breakfast?"

"Sure," she said, gesturing for him to enter the house.

"No, I meant... out?" He started rubbing the back of his neck awkwardly.

Emily squinted as she tried to understand what he was saying. Then it dawned on her and a small smile started to spread across her lips. "You mean like on a date?"

"Well, yeah," Daniel replied, squirming.

Emily smirked. She thought Daniel looked incredibly cute standing on her doorstep like that being all coy. "You're not just asking me because you feel bad about the letter?" she asked.

Daniel's expression turned horrified. "No! Not at all. I'm asking you because I like you and I—" He sighed, his words disappearing in his throat.

"I'm just joking with you," Emily replied. "I'd love to go on a date with you."

Daniel smiled and nodded, but continued standing there looking awkward.

"Did you mean right now this second?" Emily said, surprised.

"Or later?" he said hurriedly. "We could do lunch instead if you'd prefer? Or Friday night? Would you prefer Friday night?" Daniel was looking deflated.

"Daniel," Emily said, laughing, attempting to save the situation, "now is fine. I've never been on a breakfast date. It's cute."

"I went about this all the wrong way, didn't I?" Daniel said.

Emily shook her head. "No," she reassured him. "You're doing fine. But you've got to give me time to get my makeup on. Brush my hair."

"You look great as you are," Daniel said, then immediately blushed.

"I may be a liberated woman," Emily replied, "but I kind of don't want to be wearing pajamas on a date." She smiled shyly. "I won't be long."

Then she turned and trotted up the stairs with a renewed spring in her step.

*

The material of the plastic booth was sticking to the backs of Emily's legs. She fidgeted in her seat, ran her hands down the fabric of her skirt, and was reminded of a moment several months earlier when she'd been sitting across from Ben in a fancy New York restaurant willing him to propose. Only now she was sitting across from Daniel in Sunset Harbor's newest diner, a place called Joe's, sitting silently and awkwardly while Joe set their breakfast on the table.

"So," Emily said, smiling her thanks to Joe before returning her gaze to Daniel. "Here we are."

"Yup," Daniel replied, looking down into his mug. "What do you want to talk about?"

Emily laughed. "We need a subject?"

Daniel seemed instantly flummoxed. "I didn't mean we should specify. I meant that we should just, you know, talk. Chat. About stuff."

"You mean something other than the house?" Emily said with a small smile.

Daniel nodded. "Precisely."

"Well," Emily began, "how about you tell me about how long you've been playing guitar?"

"A long time," Daniel replied. "Since I was a kid. I'd say eleven at a guess."

Emily had become accustomed to Daniel's communication style, the way he would say the least number of words to convey the most amount of information. It was usually fine when they were both staring at a wall while painting it or asking the other to pass more nails. But when they were sitting opposite each other in a diner, on the other hand, it made things a little more uncomfortable.

It was clear to Emily now why Daniel had picked Sunset Harbor's new, cheap diner for their date. It was the least formal place in the world. She couldn't begin to imagine Daniel in a suit in a fancy restaurant like the ones Ben took her to.

Just then, Joe came over. "Is everything okay with your breakfasts?" he asked.

"They're fine," Emily replied, smiling courteously.

"Want a coffee top-up?" Joe added.

"Not for me, thank you," she said.

"Me neither," Daniel replied.

But instead of getting the hint and leaving them alone, Joe stayed exactly where he was, coffee pot in hand.

"You kids on a date?" he said.

Daniel looked like he wanted the ground to swallow him up. Emily couldn't help but stifle a giggle.

"Business meeting, actually," she said, sounding completely genuine.

"Oh, right, I'll leave you to it," Joe replied before wandering off with his coffee pot to pester another table of customers.

"You look like you want to get out of here," Emily said, turning her attention back to Daniel.

"Not because of you," Daniel said, looking mortified.

"Relax," Emily laughed. "I'm just teasing you. I'm feeling a bit claustrophobic in here as well." She looked over her shoulder. Joe was lingering rather close by. "Shall we go for a walk?"

He smiled. "Sure. There's a festival today down at the harbor. It's kind of cheesy."

"I like cheesy," Emily replied, sensing his hesitation.

"Cool. Well, we lower boats into the water. Happens the same time every year. The people here have turned it into a sort of celebration. I don't know, maybe you remember it from when you used to visit?"

"Actually I don't," Emily said. "I'd love to take a look."

Daniel looked shy. "I have a boat down there," he said. "Haven't used it in a long time. It's probably rusty now. I bet the motor doesn't work either."

"How come you don't use it anymore?" Emily asked.

Daniel averted his eyes. "That's another story for another day," was all he said.

Emily sensed she'd touched some kind of nerve. Their awkward date had somehow become even more awkward.

"Let's go to the festival," she said.

"Really?" Daniel asked. "We don't have to go just because of me."

"I want to," Emily replied. And she meant it. Despite the long silences and sideways glances, she enjoyed Daniel company and didn't want the date to end.

"Come on," she said brightly slapping some bills onto the table. "Hey, Joe, we've left the money for you, hope that's okay," she called out to the older man before grabbing her jacket off the back of her chair and standing.

"Emily, look, it's fine," Daniel said. "You don't have to come to some lame festival with me."

"I want to," Emily reassured him. "Honestly I do."

She began to walk toward the exit, giving Daniel no choice but to follow.

As soon as they were out on the street Emily could see the bunting and helium balloons by the harbor in the distance. The sun was out but there was a thin layer of clouds that made the air cool. Plenty of people were walking down the street heading toward the harbor and Emily realized that the lowering of the boats was indeed a big deal here. She and Daniel followed the crowds toward the harbor. A marching band was playing lively music as they walked. Lined along the sides of the streets were stalls selling cotton candy and sweets.

"Want me to get you something?" Daniel said, laughing. "That's a datelike thing to do, right?"

"I'd love that," Emily replied.

She giggled aloud as she watched Daniel weave through the crowd up to the cotton candy machine that was surrounded by children, purchase an enormous cone of blue, sparkly cotton candy for her, and carry it carefully back through the throng of people. He presented it to her with a flourish.

"What flavor is it?" Emily laughed, eyeing the fluorescent color. "I didn't know you could get sparkly blue flavor."

"I think it's grape," Daniel said.

"Sparkly grape," Emily added.

She pulled a piece of the cotton candy off. It had been about thirty years since she'd eaten one of these things and when she put the fluff in her mouth she found that it was far sweeter than she could have imagined.

"Ah, instant toothache!" she exclaimed. "Your turn."

Daniel took a handful of bright blue fluff and shoved it in his mouth. Immediately he looked disgusted.

"Oh god. People feed their children that stuff?" he said.

"Your mouth has turned blue!" Emily cried.

"So has yours," Daniel countered.

Emily laughed and looped her arm through his as they sauntered slowly down to the water's edge, their steps punctuated by the music of the marching band. As they watched the boats being lowered into the water one after the other, Emily rested her head on Daniel's shoulder. She could feel the revelry of the townspeople, and it made her reflect on how much she had grown to love this place. Wherever she looked she could see smiling faces, children running around carefree and content. She had been just like them once, before the dark events of her life had changed her forever.

"I'm sorry, this is dumb," Daniel said. "I shouldn't have brought you here. We can go if you want."

"What makes you think I want to go?" Emily replied.

"You look sad," Daniel said, shoving his hands in his pocket.

"I'm not sad," Emily replied wistfully. "I'm just thinking about life. My past." Her voice grew quieter. "And my dad."

Daniel nodded and turned his gaze back out toward the water. "Did you find what you were looking for here? Have your questions been answered?"

"I don't even know what questions I wanted answered when I came here," Emily replied without looking at him. "But I feel like in a way that letter answered them."

There was a long silence before Daniel spoke again. "Does that mean you'll be leaving then?"

He was wearing a serious expression. For the first time Emily thought she read something in his eyes. A longing. A longing for her? "I was never planning on staying," she said quietly.

Daniel looked away. "I know. But I thought you might have changed your mind."

"It's not about that," Emily replied. "It's about whether I can afford it. I'm three months into my savings already. And if Trevor Mann has his way I'll be spending the rest on legal fees and back taxes."

"I won't let that happen," Daniel said.

She paused, studied his face. "Why does it matter to you so much?"

"Because I have absolutely no legal right to be there either," Daniel said, looking at her with an expression of surprise, as if he couldn't believe she hadn't thought of it. "If you go, I go."

"Oh," Emily replied, deflated. It hadn't occurred to her that losing the plot would mean upheaval for more than just herself, that Daniel would have to go too. She'd hoped he cared about the house because of her, but maybe she'd read the situation wrong. She wondered if Daniel had anywhere else to go.

Suddenly, Emily spotted the mayor amongst the crowds. Her eyes widened mischievously. She turned from Daniel and ducked into the crowds.

"Emily, where are you going?" he said, exasperated, as he watched her go.

"Come on!" she cried, beckoning him to follow.

Emily weaved her way through groups of people as the mayor went into the general store. The bell above the door tinkled as Emily burst in after him, then again as Daniel followed behind her. The mayor turned and regarded them both.

"Hi!" she said brightly as the mayor turned to look behind him. "Do you remember me? Emily Mitchell. Emily Jane."

"Oh yes, yes," the mayor replied. "Are you enjoying the festival?"

"I am," Emily replied. "I'm glad I got to be here to see it."

The mayor smiled at her in a way that seemed to suggest he was in a hurry and wanted to get on with his day. But Emily wasn't about to budge.

"I wanted to speak to you," she said. "I wondered if you could help me."

"With what, my dear?" the mayor replied, not looking at her, reaching past her to pick up a bag of flour from the shelf.

She maneuvered herself in front of him. "Trevor Mann."

The mayor paused. "Oh?" he said, his gaze sliding over to Karen behind the counter then back to Emily. "What's he up to now?"

"He wants my land. Said there was some legal loophole with the property and that I needed a certificate of occupation."

"Well," the mayor said, looking somewhat flustered. "You know it's all about the people here. That's what matters. They're the ones that vote on these matters and you aren't exactly going out of your way to make friends."

Emily's first instinct was to refute his claim, but she realized that he was right. Other than Daniel, the only person in Sunset Harbor who was friendly with her was Rico, and he couldn't remember her name from one weekend to the next. Trevor, Karen, the mayor, none of them had reason to feel warmth toward her.

"I can't just coast off of being Roy Mitchell's daughter?" she said with a sheepish smile.

The mayor laughed. "I think you've already burned that bridge, don't you? Now, if you don't mind, I have some shopping to be getting on with."

"Of course," Emily said, moving out of the mayor's way. "Karen," she added, nodding cordially to the woman behind the till. Then she grabbed Daniel's arm and steered him out of the store.

"What was all that about?" he hissed in her ear as they exited the shop, its tinkling bell bidding them farewell.

She let go of his arm. "Daniel, I don't want to leave. I've fallen in love. With the town," she added hurriedly when she saw the flicker of panic in his eyes. "You know when you asked me if I'd found the answers I was looking for? Well, you know what, I haven't. My dad's letter didn't really answer anything. There's still so much more in that house I have to discover."

"Okay..." Daniel said, drawing the word out as though he didn't fully understand where this was going. "But what about the money situation? And Trevor Mann? I thought you said it wasn't up to you whether you stayed or not."

Emily grinned and raised her eyebrows. "I think I have an idea."

Chapter Twelve

The next day Emily woke early and went straight into town with a plan to make the people of Sunset Harbor like her. The impetus, of course, had been her desire to get them to vote for her permit; yet as she embarked, she realized she wanted to befriend them regardless. The permit was important, but whether she got it or not, what was more important to her was setting wrongs right. She finally realized how cold and standoffish she had been to everyone here, and she felt terrible. That wasn't her. Whether they voted for her or not, or became friends with her or not, she felt she had to make amends. It was time to leave the New York City Emily behind and become the friendly, small-town person she had been in her youth..

It all had to start, she realized, with Karen at the general store. She made a beeline for it and arrived just as Karen was unlocking it to begin the day.

"Oh," Karen said when she saw that it was Emily approaching. "Can you give me five minutes to get the till up and running?" Her tone wasn't hostile, but Karen was the sort of person who was overly friendly with everyone, so the lukewarm greeting was a clear sign of her dislike for Emily.

"Actually, I'm not here to buy anything," Emily said. "I wanted to speak to you."

Karen paused, her hand with the key still in the lock. "About what?"

She pushed the door open and Emily followed her inside. Karen began opening up the blinds straightaway, and buzzing around turning on lights, signs, and the till.

"Well," Emily said, following her around, feeling like she was being made to work for forgiveness, "I wanted to apologize to you. I think we got off on the wrong foot."

"We've been on the wrong foot for three months," Karen replied, quickly fastening one of the store's dark green aprons around her rotund midriff.

"I know," Emily replied. "I was a bit standoffish when I first got here because I'd just gone through a breakup and had quit my job and was kind of in a dark place. But now things are going great and I know you're an important part of this community so can we wipe the slate clean?"

Karen walked around the counter and gave Emily a look. Then finally she said, "I can but try."

"Great," Emily said brightly. "In that case, this is for you."

Karen narrowed her eyes as she looked at the small envelope Emily was holding out. She took it suspiciously. "What is it?"

"An invitation. I'm holding a dinner party at the house. I thought the townsfolk might be interested in seeing how I've renovated it. I'm going to cook, make cocktails. It will be fun."

Karen looked bemused but took the invitation nonetheless.

"Don't feel like you have to RSVP right away," Emily said. "Bye!"

She rushed out of the general store and headed along the streets toward her next location. As she walked, she realized how much she'd grown to love the town. It truly was beautiful, with its cute architecture, flower baskets, and tree-lined streets. The bunting was still up from the festival, making it look like a continuous celebration was taking place.

Emily's next stop was the gas station. She'd avoided it thus far, pretending to herself it was just because she hadn't needed to do much driving since arriving here, but in reality it was because she had not wanted to run into the man who'd given her a lift when she first arrived at Sunset Harbor. She'd been the rudest to him out of everyone but if she was trying to make good with the people of Sunset Harbor, he had to be on her guest list. Since he owned the only gas station in town, he was known by absolutely everyone. If she could get a good word in with him, maybe the rest of them would follow suit.

"Hi," she said tentatively as she opened the door to the shop and peeked her head around. "It's Birk, isn't it?"

"Ah," the man said. "If it isn't the mysterious stranger who appeared in the snowstorm never to be seen again."

"That's me," Emily said, noting that he seemed to be wearing exactly the same pair of greasy jeans as he had been the first time they'd met. "I've been here the whole time, actually."

"You have?" Birk said. "I figured you'd moved on months ago. You spent the whole winter in that drafty old house?"

"Yes," Emily said. "Only it's not drafty anymore. I've been fixing the place up." There was an air of pride in her tone.

"Well, I'll be damned," the man said. "Only," he added, "you might've waited before doing any big repairs. You know there's a storm coming tonight? Worst one to hit Maine in a hundred years."

"Oh no," Emily said. She hadn't thought anything could harm her buoyant mood, but fate always seemed to throw things her way that would bring her crashing back down to reality. "I wanted to apologize for being rude when we first met. I don't think I ever properly thanked you for getting me out of such a dire situation. I was still in my New York mode, although that's no excuse. I hope you can forgive me."

"Don't mention it," Birk said. "I didn't do it for your thanks, I did it 'cause you needed help."

"I know," Emily replied. "But please accept my thanks all the same."

Birk nodded. He seemed like a prideful kind of man, one who didn't accept gratitude easily. "So are you planning on staying much longer?"

"Another three months if I can afford it," Emily said. "Although Trevor Mann on the zoning board is doing his hardest to get me evicted so he can take over the grounds."

At the mention of his name, Birk rolled his eyes. "Ugh, don't worry about Trevor Mann. He's run for mayor every year for the last thirty and no one's ever voted for him. Between you and me, I think he has a Napoleon complex."

Emily laughed. "Thanks, that makes me feel a lot better." She rummaged in her satchel and pulled out one of her party invitations. "Birk, I'm going to hold a dinner party up at the house for people in the town to come to. I don't suppose you and your wife would want to come?" She held the envelope out to him.

Birk looked at it, a little bemused. Emily wondered when the last time was that the man had been invited to a dinner party, or whether he ever had.

"Well, that's very kind of you," Birk said, taking the letter and slipping it into the big pocket of his jeans. "I think I might just come along. We love a celebration here. You might have noticed the bunting."

"I did," Emily replied. "I was at the harbor for the boat show. It was great."

"You came?" Birk said, looking even more bemused than he had before.

"Yup," Emily said with a smile. "Hey, I wonder if you'd be able to do me a favor? I need to hurry home if I want to stormproof the house before the evening but I've still got tons of invites to deliver. I don't suppose you'd be able to pass them on to the recipients when they come in for gas?"

She felt bad asking such a huge favor of Birk, but the impending storm was going to derail her plan for handing out the invitations. There definitely wasn't time to hand them out individually to each person she wanted to attend the party. But if she didn't get home and prepare the house for the storm, there wouldn't be anywhere for her to host a party for the townsfolk anyway!

Birk let out a big belly laugh. If he hadn't been invited to a dinner party for years, he certainly hadn't been integral to one's organization before! "Well, let me see?" Who's on your list?" Emily handed him the envelopes and he thumbed through. "Dr. Patel, yes she'll be in after her shift. Cynthia from the bookstore, Charles and Barbara Bradshaw, yes, yes, all these people will be in sooner or later." He looked up and smiled. "I can hand these out for you."

"Thank you so much, Birk," Emily said. "I owe you one. See you around?"

Birk waved as she turned to leave then let out one of his small chuckles as he looked through the delicate party invitations she'd entrusted to him. "Oh, Emily. Why don't you put one of these up on the town bulletin board? Most folks look it over on a daily basis. You'll get more guests that way as well, since there's only a select few here. Assuming you want more guests."

"I do!" Emily exclaimed. "I want to make good with as many people as possible. I feel like I haven't integrated with you guys at all, and I really want to get to know you all. Make some friends here."

Birk looked touched, although he was doing his best to hide his emotion. "Well, doing up that old house is certainly one way of going about it. Anybody around here would want to see the fixed up house."

"Okay. I'll put up a flyer on the bulletin board then if you think it will help. Thanks, Birk." Emily was grateful that he was helping her out. Just like when he'd picked her up that night in the snowstorm all those months ago, he was willing to go out of his way to help someone else. She smiled to herself, looking forward to getting to know him better.

"Don't be a stranger, you hear me?" Birk added as she slipped through the door.

"I won't!" Emily called back inside before shutting the door.

She rushed up to the town bulletin board and grabbed a pen and piece of paper, then along with the other notices on the board, she wrote up a flyer for her party and pinned it up on the board. She just prayed that whoever came had the courtesy to RSVP to the invite so at the very least she'd know how many people she needed to cook for.

Once the invite was up, she jumped in her car and headed home to warn Daniel of the impending storm and to prepare the house for its arrival.

She found him in the ballroom. It was starting to look amazing in there. The Tiffany windows made colors streak across the walls, which were made even more beautiful, if such a thing was possible, by the crystal chandelier they had cleaned and hung up. Walking into the ballroom felt like stepping into the deep blue sea, into a dreamland.

"I just heard from town that there's a bad storm coming," Emily told Daniel.

He stopped what he was doing. "How bad?"

"What do you mean how bad?" Emily said, exasperated.

"I mean is it going to be 'batten down the hatches' bad?"

"I think so," she said.

"Okay. We should board up the windows."

It felt strange to Emily, putting the plywood back up over the windows when three months earlier they'd worked together to remove them. So much had changed since then between them. Working on the house together had bonded them. Their shared love of the place had pulled them together. That, and the pain they both shared over the disappearance of Emily's father.

Once the house was ready, and the first fat raindrops began to splotch on the ground, Emily noticed that Daniel kept peering out of a gap in the plywood.

"You're not thinking of going back to the carriage house, are you?" she asked. "Because this house is way sturdier. It must have already survived a bad storm or two in its time. Not like your flimsy little carriage house."

"My carriage house is not flimsy," Daniel contested with a smirk.

Just then, the heavens opened and a sheet of rain began to thunder down on the house. The sound was phenomenal, like pounding drums.

"Wow," Emily said, raising her eyebrows. "I've never heard anything like that before."

The percussion of rain was accompanied by a sudden gust of screaming wind. Daniel peered out the gap again and Emily suddenly realized that he was looking over at the barn.

"You're worried about the darkroom, aren't you?" she asked.

"Yeah," Daniel replied with a sigh. "It's funny. I haven't been in there for years but the thought of it being destroyed by the storm makes me sad."

Suddenly, Emily remembered the stray dog she'd met when she'd been in there. "Oh my God!" she cried.

Daniel looked at her, concerned. "What's wrong?"

"There's a dog, a stray who lives in the barn. We can't leave it out in the storm! What if the barn comes down and crushes him?" Emily began to panic at the thought.

"It's okay," Daniel said. "I'll go get him. You stay here."

"No," Emily said, tugging on his arm. "You shouldn't go out there."

"Then you want to leave the dog?"

Emily was torn. She didn't want Daniel to put himself in any danger, but at the same time she couldn't leave the helpless dog out there in the storm.

"Let's get the dog," Emily replied. "But I'm coming with you."

Emily found some raincoats and boots and the two of them suited up. As Emily opened the back door a bolt of lightning cracked through the sky. She gasped at the magnitude of it, then heard the enormous rumble of thunder in the air.

"I think it's right over us," she called back to Daniel, her voice eaten up by the roar of the storm.

"Then we've picked a great time to head out into it!" came his sarcastic response.

The two of them trudged across the lawn, churning the neatly manicured grass into mud. Emily knew how much Daniel cared about his yard and knew it must be killing him to know he was damaging it with every one of his heavy footsteps.

As the rain lashed against Emily's face, making it sting, a flash of a memory hit her with a force much stronger than the winds that whipped around her. She remembered being a very young girl, out with Charlotte in a storm. Their dad had warned them not to go too far from home, but Emily had persuaded her younger sister to go just a bit further. Then the storm had come and they'd gotten lost. They'd both been terrified, crying, wailing as the winds battered their little bodies. They'd been clinging to each other, their hands locked, but the rain had made them slippery and at some point she'd lost hold of Charlotte.

Emily froze on the spot as the memory flashed through her mind's eye. She felt like she was back there, reliving that moment when she'd been a terrified seven-year-old girl, remembering that awful expression on her dad's face when she'd told him Charlotte was gone, that she'd lost her out in the storm.

"Emily!" Daniel shouted, his voice almost entirely swallowed up by the wind. "Come on!"

She turned her attention back to the moment and followed Daniel.

Finally they made it to the barn, feeling like they'd trudged across a vast swampy wilderness to get there. The roof had already been blown off by the force of the wind and Emily didn't have much hope for the rest of it.

She showed Daniel the hole and together they squeezed inside. Rain continued to lash on them through the gaping exposed roof and Emily looked around to see that the barn was filling with water.

"Where did you find the dog?" Daniel called to Emily. Despite the raincoat he looked like he was soaked to the bone, and his hair stuck to his face in tendrils.

"It was over here," she said, beckoning to the dark corner of the barn where she'd seen the dog's head when she left it.

But when they got to the place Emily thought the dog would be, they were met with a surprise.

"Oh my god," Emily squealed. "Puppies!"

Daniel's eyes widened in disbelief as he looked at the pink, naked, writhing pups. They were newborn, possibly even less than a day old.

"What are we going to do with them all?" Daniel said, his eyes as round as moons.

"Put them in our pockets?" Emily replied.

There were five puppies in all. They popped one in each pocket and then Emily cradled the runt in her hands. Daniel saw to the mama dog, who was snapping at them both for having disturbed her puppies.

The walls of the barn were shaking as they walked back to the hole with the squirming puppies in their pockets.

As they walked back through the barn, Emily could see the damage the rain was doing to everything inside, and she realized that it would surely be destroyed—the boxes of her father's photo albums, Daniel's teenage photography, the aged equipment that might be worth something to a collector. The thought broke her heart. Though she'd already taken one box into the main house, there were still three more filled with her dad's photo albums inside the barn. She couldn't bear to lose all those precious memories.

Against better sense, Emily rushed over to where she'd found the stack of boxes. She knew that there was a mixture of Daniel's pictures and her dad's in the boxes, and the top one she found was one filled with her dad's photo albums. She popped the runt on the top of the box and heaved it into her arms.

"Emily," Daniel called. "What are you doing? We need to get out before this whole place falls down!"

"I'm coming," she called back. "I just don't want to leave them."

She tried to find a way to take another box, stacking it below the first and wedging them both between her chin, but it was too heavy and cumbersome. There was no way she would be able to rescue all the boxes of photographs.

Daniel came over. He set the mama dog onto the floor, then tied a leash for her from some rope. Then he grabbed two more boxes of Emily's family photos. They now had all three of her dad's remaining boxes of photographs, but not a single one of Daniel's.

"What about yours?" Emily cried.

"Yours are more important," Daniel replied stoically.

"Only for me," Emily replied. "What about—"

Before she could finish her sentence the barn made a terrifying creaking noise.

"Come on," Daniel said. "We have to go."

Emily didn't get the chance to protest. Daniel was already charging from the barn, his arms laden with her precious family photographs at the expense of his own. His sacrifice touched her and she couldn't help wondering why he would go out of his way to put her needs above his own.

As they ducked back out through the gap in the barn, the rain lashed against them fiercer than ever. Emily could hardly move the wind was so strong. She battled against it, making her way slowly across the lawn.

Suddenly, an almighty crash came from behind. Emily squealed with shock and looked back to see that the large oak tree at the side of the property had ripped out of the ground and smashed into the barn. Had the tree fallen just a minute earlier, they would both have been crushed.

"That was a little bit close for comfort," Daniel yelled. "We'd better get back inside as quickly as we can."

They made it across the lawn and to the back door. When Emily pulled it open, the wind ripped it off its hinges and flung it far across the yard.

"Quick, into the living room," Emily said, shutting the door that separated the kitchen from the living room.

She was dripping wet and making huge streaks of rain water across the floorboards. They went to the living room and put the dog and its puppies on the rug beside the hearth.

"Can you start a fire?" Emily asked Daniel. "They must be freezing." She rubbed her hands together to get the circulation going again. "I know I am."

Without a single complaint, Daniel got straight to work. A moment later a blazing fire warmed the room.

Emily helped the puppies find their mama. One by one they began to suckle, relaxing into their new environment. But one of the puppies didn't join in.

"I think this one's sick," Emily said concerned.

"It's the runt," Daniel said. "It probably won't make it through the night."

Emily felt tearful at the thought. "What are we going to do with them all?" she said.

"I'll rebuild the barn for them."

Emily laughed in mock derision. "You've never had a pet before, have you?"

"How did you guess?" Daniel replied jovially.

Suddenly, Emily noticed that there was blood on Daniel's top. It was coming from a gash in his forehead.

"Daniel, you're bleeding!" she cried.

Daniel touched his forehead then looked at the blood on his fingers. "I think I was snagged by one of the branches. It's nothing, just a superficial wound."

"Let me put something on it so it doesn't get infected."

Emily went into the kitchen to search for the first-aid kit. Thanks to the wind coming in through the space where the back door used to be, it was much harder to move around the kitchen than she thought it would be. Wind was racing around the room, throwing any item not bolted down to the ground all over the place. Emily tried not to think of the devastation or how much it would cost to fix.

Finally she found the first-aid kit and went back to the living room.

The mama dog had stopped whimpering and all of the puppies were feeding except for the runt. Daniel was holding it in his hands, trying to coax it to feed. Something about the sight of him made her heart stir. Daniel continued to surprise her—from his ability to cook, to his fine taste in music, his talented guitar playing, and his handiness with a hammer to this, his gentle care over a helpless creature.

"No luck?" Emily asked.

He shook his head. "It's not looking good for the little guy."

"We should name it," Emily said. "It shouldn't die without a name."

"We don't know whether it's a boy or girl."

"Then we should call it something gender neutral."

"What, like Alex?" Daniel said, frowning with confusion.

Emily laughed. "No, I meant more like Rain."

Daniel shrugged. "Rain. That works." He put Rain back with the other pups. They were all clambering to be close to their mom, and the runt kept getting pushed out. "What about the rest of them?"

"Well," Emily said. "How about Storm, Cloud, Wind, and Thunder."

Daniel grinned. "Very appropriate. And the mama?"

"Why don't you name her?" Emily said. She'd already gotten to name all the puppies.

Daniel stroked the mama dog's head. She made a content sound. "How about Mogsy?"

Emily burst out laughing. "That's not very on theme!"

Daniel just shrugged. "It's my choice, right? I choose Mogsy."

Emily smirked. "Sure. Your choice. Mogsy it is. Now, let me look at that wound."

She sat on the couch, guiding Daniel's head toward her with gentle fingers. She swept the hair from his brow and began to disinfect the gash across his forehead. He was right in that it wasn't deep, but it was bleeding profusely. Emily used several Band-Aids to hold the wound together.

"If you're lucky," she said, sticking another piece on, "you'll have a cool scar."

Daniel smirked. "Great. Girls love scars, right?"

Emily laughed. She stuck the last strip in place. But instead of moving away, her fingers lingered there, against his flesh. She swept a stray piece of hair away from his eyes, then traced her fingertips down the contour of his face, down to his lips.

Daniel's eyes smoldered into hers. He reached up and took her hand then pressed a kiss into her palm.

He grabbed her then, pulling her down from the settee and into his lap. Their drenched clothes pressed together as he pressed his mouth into hers. Her hands roved all over him, feeling every part of him. The heat between them ignited as they peeled one another's wet clothing from their bodies, then sunk against one another, moving in a harmonious rhythm, their minds so consumed with one another that they no longer noticed the storm that raged outside.

Chapter Thirteen

Emily woke tangled in Daniel's limbs. The sun was shining fiercely, making it seem like the storm hadn't happened at all. But Emily knew it had, and she knew the damage would be extensive.

She untangled herself from Daniel's octopus-like grip and slipped on a thin camisole dress, then went downstairs to inspect the damage.

In the living room, Mogsy had clearly had a bit of a freakout during the storm. One of the cushions was all chewed up, the stuffing strewn around the room. The rug was also badly stained from her and Daniel's discarded, muddy, wet clothes. She smiled to herself at the memory of the way they'd peeled them off one another.

Well, if a muddy rug and a chewed up cushion are the only things that got ruined then I've done pretty well, she thought.

The biggest surprise to Emily was that Rain the runt puppy had survived the night and was suckling happily. But that also meant she now had a dog and five puppies to look after. She had no idea what she was going to do with them all, but figured she'd deal with that later—after she prepared some leftover chicken for Mogsy, who was probably hungry. And after she focused on the house.

She heard Daniel stirring upstairs as she continued to do her rounds of the house. When she passed through the dining room toward the ballroom entrance, she heard Daniel's footsteps pattering up behind her.

"Is it bad?" he asked.

Though he'd never expressly said it, Emily knew that of all the rooms in the house the ballroom was Daniel's favorite. It was the grandest, the most magical, and the room that had first brought them together, had sparked this whole thing. Without the ballroom, last night might never have happened. To think that anything might have happened to it was dreadful for them both.

Emily looked inside tentatively. Daniel was close behind.

"It looks okay," Emily said. But then she noticed something glittering on the floor and rushed over. Her suspicions were confirmed when she picked it up and saw it was a shard of glass. "Oh no," she cried. "Not the Tiffany window. Please, not the Tiffany window!"

Together she and Daniel pulled down the plywood covering the antique windows. As they did, more shards fell, shattering onto the floor.

"I can't believe it," Emily wailed, knowing that it would cost too much to replace, that it was indeed irreplaceable.

"I know someone who might be able to help," Daniel said, trying to cheer her up.

"For free?" she said glumly, hopelessly.

Daniel shrugged. "You never know. He might do it just for the love of it."

Emily knew he was trying to make her feel better, but she couldn't help but feel tearful. "It's a big job," she said.

"And the people here are good," Daniel said. He took her by the shoulders. "Come on, there's nothing we can do at the moment anyway. Let me make you breakfast."

He steered her into the kitchen by her shoulders, but it too was in bad shape. Daniel and Emily picked up strewn items, then Emily put the coffee on to brew, grateful that the coffee pot hadn't succumbed to the same fate of smashing against the floor like the toaster had.

"How do you feel about waffles?" Daniel asked her.

"I feel pretty good about waffles," Emily replied as she sat down at the breakfast table. "But I don't have a waffle iron, do I?"

"Well, technically you do," Daniel replied. When Emily frowned he went on to further explain. "Serena reserved it at the garage sale. Said she'd come back and pay for it another time. I couldn't tell if she was joking or not but she never came back so I guess she didn't really want it." He came over and plopped a steaming cup of black coffee in front of Emily.

"Thanks," Emily said, feeling a little shy about the innate intimacy of Daniel cooking her breakfast.

As she sipped her coffee and watched Daniel cooking, spatula in hand, she felt reborn. It was not just the house that had been transformed overnight; she had too. Her memory of their lovemaking was itself hazy, but she could remember the feeling of ecstasy that had rippled through her body. It had almost been an out-of-body experience. She squirmed in her seat just thinking about it.

Leaving the waffles to cook, Daniel sat opposite her and took a sip of his own coffee.

"I don't think I've said good morning properly yet," he said. He leaned across the table and took her face in his hands. But before he got a chance to plant a kiss on her lips, a shrill beeping noise shattered the moment.

Emily and Daniel sprang apart.

"What the hell is that?" Emily exclaimed, holding her ears.

"It's the fire alarm!" Daniel yelled, looking back to the counter where the waffle iron was spewing out clouds of black smoke.

Emily leapt up from her seat as sparks began to fly into the air. Daniel was quick to take action, grabbing a tea towel to smother the flames.

Smoke billowed around the room, making Daniel and Emily cough.

"I guess Serena won't be coming back for her waffle iron after all," Emily said.

*

After breakfast, they set to work fixing up the house. Daniel went up on the roof to inspect it.

"Well?" Emily asked hopefully once he climbed back down from the attic.

"It seems to be okay," Daniel said. "There is some damage. Hard to tell. We won't really know how bad it is until the next big storm rips through. Then, unfortunately, we might find out the hard way." He sighed. "As long as there isn't another storm anytime soon I think you'll get away with it."

"Fingers crossed," Emily said, thinly.

"What's wrong?" Daniel asked, picking up on her downbeat mood.

"I'm just finding it a bit depressing," Emily said. "Walking around the house working out what's broken or damaged. Why don't we work on the grounds instead? At least the sun is shining."

It was a beautiful day. The storm seemed to have chased away spring, leaving summer in its wake.

"I've got an idea," Daniel said. "I haven't shown you the rose garden I planted yet, have I?"

"No," Emily said. "I'd like to see it."

"It's this way."

He took her by the hand and led her out across the grounds then over the single-track road toward the ocean path. As they strolled down the pebbled slope, Emily caught sight of the ocean. The view was breathtaking.

There was a clump of vegetation ahead of them that looked like it would lead to nothing but an overgrown patch. But Daniel led her straight to it, then swiped back a large branch.

"It's a little hidden out of the way. Careful your clothes don't snag."

Curious, Emily ducked in through the opening Daniel had created. What she saw as she emerged on the other side made her breath catch in her lungs. Roses, in every conceivable color, were everywhere. Red, yellow, pink, white, even black. If stepping into the ballroom and seeing the light through the Tiffany glass had been awe-inspiring, this was even better.

Emily twirled in a circle, feeling more alive and free than she had in years.

"It survived the storm," Daniel said as he emerged through the foliage behind her. "I wasn't sure it would."

Emily turned and threw her arms around him, letting her tousled hair fall down her back. "It's incredible. How did you keep this a secret from me?"

Daniel held onto her tightly, breathing in the scent of her as it mixed with the pungent perfume of roses. "It's not like I take all the girls I date here."

Emily moved back slightly so she could gaze into his eyes. "Is that what we're doing? Dating?"

Daniel raised an eyebrow and smirked. "You tell me," he said suggestively.

Emily rose onto her tiptoes and pressed a gentle, tender kiss against his lips. "Does that answer your question?" she asked dreamily.

She moved out of his embrace and began to look around the rose garden more carefully. The colors were amazing.

"How long has this been here?" she asked in awe.

"Well," Daniel said, settling himself to the ground in a small clearing, "I planted it after I came back from Tennessee. Gardening and photography. I wasn't particularly masculine in my youth," he added with a laugh.

"Well, you're all man now," Emily replied with a grin. She went over to where Daniel was sitting languorously stretched out like a cat, shards of sunlight and shadow dappling his skin. She lay down beside him and rested her head in the crook of his neck, feeling sleepy, like she could have a nap right here. "When were you in Tennessee?" she asked.

"It wasn't a good part of my life," Daniel said, his tone betraying to her that he felt very uncomfortable talking about it. Daniel had always been very private, talking very little about himself. He was more of a doer, a practical person. Chatting, particularly about emotionally charged subjects, was not his forte. But Emily shared that with him. Expressing herself was something she struggled with as well. "I was young," Daniel continued. "Twenty years old. I was dumb."

"Did something happen?" Emily asked, gently, careful not to scare him away. Her hand was on his chest, tracing up and down the fabric of his shirt, feeling the muscles beneath.

When Daniel spoke, she could hear him through the ear she had resting on his chest, and his voice sent vibrations rumbling through her.

"I did something I'm not proud of," he said. "I did it for a good reason but that doesn't make it okay."

"What did you do?" Emily asked. She was certain that whatever he said would in no way diminish her blossoming feelings for him.

"I was arrested in Tennessee. For assaulting a man. I had a girlfriend. But she had a husband."

"Oh," Emily said, as it dawned on her where this conversation might be going. "And I'm guessing the husband was the man you assaulted?"

"Yes," Daniel replied. "He was violent. Harassing her, you know? She'd kicked him out way before I met her but this guy would keep coming around. It was getting scary. The cops weren't doing anything."

"What did you do?" Emily asked.

"Well, the next time he came around, threatening her to kill her, I taught him a lesson. Made sure he would never show up on her doorstep again. I beat him up. He ended up in the hospital."

Emily winced at the thought of Daniel pummeling someone so bad they had to be hospitalized. She could hardly marry all the versions of Daniel up in her mind: the sensitive, misunderstood runaway photographer, the young, dumb thug, and the man who planted a garden of multicolored roses. But then the person she'd been just a few months ago when she was Ben's girlfriend was completely different from the person she was now. Despite the old adage that people never changed, her experience of life had been the opposite: people always changed.

"Thing is," Daniel said, "she broke up with me after that. Said I scared her. He played the victim and she went back to him. He had such a hold over her that after everything, he was able to manipulate her right back to where he wanted her. I felt so betrayed."

"You shouldn't feel betrayed. Her going back to him was more about his control over her than her love for you. I should know. I—" Emily lost her voice. She had never spoken to anyone about what she was going to speak to Daniel about. Not even Amy. "I know what it's like," she finally said. "I was in an emotionally abusive relationship once."

Daniel looked stunned.

"I don't like talking about it," Emily added. "I was young too, still a teenager, in fact. Everything was great until I was heading off to college. I thought I was in love with him. We'd been together for over a year, which seemed like such a big deal at the time. But when I said I wanted to study out of state, something in him shifted. He became very jealous, seemed convinced I would cheat on him as soon as I left. I broke up with him because of how terribly he was behaving, but he threatened to kill himself if I didn't take him back. That's how it starts, the manipulation. The control. I ended up staying with him out of fear."

"Did he stop you going out of state to college?"

"Yes," she said. "I gave up one of my goals because of him, even though he treated me like shit. And you know what's happening is crazy but you play all these psychological tricks on yourself, rewriting situations you know in your heart aren't right but telling yourself that it's a sign of how much you're loved. To everyone on the outside it looks like insanity. When it's over, it looks like insanity to you too. But when you're there, living it, you find ways to make it make sense."

"What happened to him in the end?"

"Well, funnily enough, *he* cheated on *me*. I was devastated at the time but it didn't take me long to see how it was such a blessing in disguise. I dread to think what could have happened if he hadn't ended it with me. I would have been stuck with him for however long he wanted me around, and whatever damage he'd already done to me would have become even more entrenched."

They both fell silent. Daniel stroked her hair.

"Do you want to go up to the rocky coastline with me?" he said suddenly.

"Sure," Emily said, a little surprised by the suggestion but excited at the same time. "How do we get there?"

"We take the bike."

"The bike? Your motorcycle?" Emily stammered.

Emily had never been on a motorcycle. The thought terrified and excited her in equal measure.

They went back through the rose garden and across the driveway to the carriage house. Daniel retrieved his motorcycle from the garage, one of the outbuildings that had thankfully survived the storm. While he prepared the bike for the trip, Emily checked on Mogsy and her pups. Rain was still clinging on to life. She coaxed him to his mother's nipple and stroked the stray's head. Mogsy looked up at her with big, grateful eyes, then licked Emily's hand. It was almost as if she was thanking Emily for rescuing her from the storm, while apologizing for having nipped at her in fear when she'd thought Emily was stealing her new babies. Emily felt like there was a moment of understanding between them, and for the first time since rescuing the dog, she felt like maybe she could keep her around in her life. Maybe taking care of another living being was exactly what had been missing in Emily's life.

"You're doing great," she said to Mogsy. "Now get some sleep. I'll be back a bit later."

Mogsy made a satisfied whining noise, then let her head sink onto her front paws.

As Emily gently shut the door to the living room, she heard the sound of an engine kicking into life and rushed outside. Daniel was there on the motorcycle grinning at her. Emily jumped on the back and wrapped her arms around him. Daniel twisted the throttle and the bike roared away.

*

Wind whipped through Emily's hair. She felt free and alive. The sunshine was warm against her skin. The rocky coastline was beautiful, providing a whole new angle to Sunset Harbor she'd never seen before. She loved it, being up here, tasting the sea air, smelling the blossom trees, hearing the distant crashing waves.

"This is incredible!" Emily cried, feeling giddy with excitement.

Daniel drove her all the way along the cliff path, then they were soaring downhill, racing at a speed that made Emily's stomach flip.

He drove them all the way along the coast path, then steered into the marina. As soon as the bike stopped, he helped her off.

"Fun?" he asked, squeezing her fingers.

"Exhilarating," Emily replied with a grin. Then she looked around her at the marina. "You know, I've never been here before," she said.

"It's where my boat is kept," Daniel said. "Come on."

She followed him along the marina path, past rowboats and speedboats that were tied up. Right at the end, there was a small, rusted boat looking forlorn and uncared for.

"This is yours?" Emily asked.

Daniel nodded. "Not much to look at, I know. I can't bring myself to fix it and put it back in the water."

"Why?" Emily asked.

Daniel didn't speak for a long time. Eventually he just said, "I really don't know." Then he looked back at her. "We should probably head back to the house. I can fix the kitchen door for you."

Emily gently touched his arm, keeping him in place. "Will you let me help you? With the boat? I can take some of my savings."

Daniel looked genuinely shocked—and touched.

"No one has ever offered to pay for something for me before," he said.

The thought of that saddened her.

"Thank you," he said. "That means a lot. But I can't accept it."

"But I want to," Emily told him. "You've helped me so much. I mean you could be fixing your boat right now instead of coming home to fix my door! Please. Let me help you. What do you need? A new engine? A coat of paint? We could make it our next project. First fix the house, then fix the boat?"

Daniel looked away, not meeting her eye. Emily could tell that something was on his mind. He gave a little shrug and put his hands in his pockets. Then he looked back at the bike, as though indicating silently that he was ready to leave this place, that he was done thinking about his boat and the state of disrepair he'd allowed it to get into.

Finally he spoke, his words coming out in one long, heavy exhalation.

"I just don't know if either will be enough to fix ourselves."

Chapter Fourteen

Arms laden with groceries, Emily struggled to the car and dumped them in the trunk. It was the night of the party. She'd had twenty RSVPs and found that she was more excited to be a hostess than she'd expected she would be. She'd woken up early that morning to get the beef stew cooking in the slow cooker. The desserts were already done; she'd made them late last night and they were sitting in the fridge to set overnight. Which meant once she got home all she had to do was decorate and whip up the vegetarian option of risotto an hour before the guests arrived.

She smiled to herself as she drove back home, relishing the opportunity to organize and plan, something she'd been denied the chance to do during her seven-year relationship with Ben.

When she pulled up into the drive, she noticed that Daniel wasn't on the grounds anywhere. She grabbed her groceries from the trunk and went inside, then dumped them on the kitchen table. She listened but couldn't hear the sounds of hammering or drilling coming from anywhere in the house. It was unusual for Daniel not to be around but Emily shrugged it off and got to work decorating the house. She put candles everywhere, then fresh flowers in vases on both the coffee table and the dining table, the two rooms she was planning on hosting the party in, though she made sure the kitchen looked up to scratch as well, knowing how people tended to migrate around it at soirees, particularly when in search for more alcohol. She hung homemade bunting around the living room, put a large glass bowl of potpourri in the bathroom, and set the table with the finest silver—pieces of value she'd salvaged from amongst the hoards of junk. She poured red wine into the six beautiful crystal decanters she'd salvaged from a cupboard in the kitchen.

Emily relocated the puppies to the back utility room so she could use the living room for the party. Her plan was for socializing and aperitifs in the living room, then a dinner in the dining room.

The clock reached 5 p.m. so she got to work making the risotto. As she entered the kitchen, the smells of the stew that had been slow cooking all day wafted up her nostrils and made her salivate. She'd gotten out of the habit of spending time cooking meals when she'd been with Ben—he preferred to go out for dinner—and was thoroughly enjoying it now. Twenty people was a lot to cook for, though, so it was a little stressful to get the quantities and timing right. But with the vast kitchen and all its gadgets at her disposal, it wasn't as bad as she'd worried it could be. She just wondered about

Daniel. He was supposed to be here helping her fix the dinner; he was the self-proclaimed foodie, after all. But every time she peered out the window, there was no sign of him. Not on the grounds, nor in the carriage house that sat in darkness.

When she was done, she went up to her room and changed. It felt strange dolling herself up after so many months without having even worn a lick of eyeliner, but she enjoyed the old rituals. She went for a striking look with bold, crimson lips and dark lashes that brought out the color in her eyes. The dress she'd chosen was electric blue and figure hugging. She had matching heels, then rounded the whole ensemble off with a silver cuff necklace. Outfit complete, she stepped back and admired herself in the mirror. She'd completely transformed herself and laughed with delight.

It was 6.45 p.m. so she lit all the scented candles to give the smell time to permeate through the house, then checked on the stew and the risotto.

Once everything was ready, Emily looked around again for Daniel. She went and checked the carriage house but he wasn't there. That's when she noticed his motorcycle wasn't in the garage. He must have gone out for another ride.

Great timing, she thought, staring at the clock. He was supposed to be here. She didn't want to be clingy but she still couldn't help but worry, especially when Daniel still wasn't back when the first guests arrived.

Emily had to put him out of her mind and put on her game face instead.

She opened the door to find Charles Bradshaw from the fish restaurant and his wife, Barbara, on the steps. He handed her a bottle of red wine; she handed her flowers.

"This is very kind of you," Emily said.

"I really can't believe my eyes," Charles said, glancing all around him. "You've restored the place so beautifully. And so quickly."

"It's not finished yet," Emily said. "But thank you."

She took their coats and led them into the living room, where there were more appreciative gasps. Before she had a chance to offer them anything to drink, the doorbell rang again. People in Sunset Harbor were pretty prompt, it seemed.

She opened the door and saw Birk standing there, alone. He apologized for his wife, who was feeling under the weather. Then he said, "It's really true. It wasn't your ghost that came to visit me in my gas station. You really did last up here by yourself!" He started laughing and grabbed her hand to shake.

"I can hardly believe it myself," Emily said with a laugh. She was going to add that she hadn't been by herself, that she'd had Daniel's help all along, but since he wasn't here, the words somehow didn't leave her mouth. She realized then that she felt let down by him for not being here.

Emily led Birk into the living room. She didn't need to introduce him; he already knew Charles and Barbara.

The doorbell rang again and Emily opened the door to find Cynthia standing there. Cynthia owned a small bookstore in town. She had bright red curly hair and always wore clothes that clashed terribly with it. Tonight she was in a strange lime green and purple ensemble that did nothing to flatter her slightly overweight frame, with bright red lipstick and bright green nail polish. Emily knew that Cynthia had a reputation for being outspoken and slightly outrageous but had invited her anyway out of goodwill. Maybe she'd provide a source of entertainment to the other guests if she really did live up to the rumors!

"Emily!" Cynthia exclaimed, her voice so shrill it was painful.

"Hello, Cynthia," Emily replied. "Thanks so much for coming."

"Well, you know what the locals say in Sunset Harbor. 'It's not a party without Cynthia.'"

Emil suspected that such a statement had never been uttered by a single person in Sunset Harbor. She gestured for Cynthia to join the others in the living room, then heard a squeal of excitement as Cynthia greeted the other guests with equal enthusiasm and volume.

The doorbell rang again and when Emily answered she saw Doctor Sunita Patel and her husband, Raj, at the doorstep. A little way behind them, Serena was helping Rico along the garden path.

"I saw the tree on your lawn," Doctor Patel said, kissing Emily's cheek and handing her a bottle of wine. "The storm hit us pretty badly as well."

"Oh, I know," Emily replied. "It was pretty frightening."

Raj shook Emily's hand. "Nice to meet you. I'm a landscaper, by the way, so if you want me to take care of that fallen tree for you I'm more than happy. Just pop in anytime. I own the nursery in town."

Emily had walked past the beautiful garden store with its gorgeous flower displays and hanging baskets many times during her trips into town. She'd wanted to go inside on more than one occasion to check out all the bird baths, sundials, and pre-grown topiaries but hadn't yet gotten the chance.

"You'd do that?" Emily asked, taken aback by the generosity. "That would be amazing."

"It's the least I can do considering you're opening up your home for us."

Raj and Sunita went into the living room and Emily turned her attention to Serena and Rico, who had almost reached the doorstep. Serena looked beautiful in a black dress with a scooped back and gold choker, her black hair hanging in loose waves, her lips a beautiful red.

"We made it!" she grinned, reaching an arm out around Emily's neck and hugging her.

"I'm so glad," Emily said. "You're pretty much the only person here who I actually know."

"Oh really?" Serena said, laughing. "What about Mr. Beefcake?"

Emily shook her head. "Oh God, don't even mention him right now."

Serena pulled a face. Emily laughed and turned her attention to Rico.

"Thanks for coming, Rico," she said. "I'm really happy to see you."

"It's just nice to get out of the house at my age, Ellie."

"Emily," Serena corrected.

"That's what I said," Rico replied.

Serena rolled her eyes, and the two of them stepped into the hallway. Emily didn't get a chance to close the door behind her because she saw Karen parking up along the street. Of all the people whose RSVPs she'd been skeptical over, Karen's had been the main one. But maybe the fact that Emily had done all the grocery shopping for the party at Karen's store had swayed the woman and won her over. It had been a pretty huge sum of money to spend at a small, local store.

Then right behind Karen, Emily saw the town mayor. She hadn't had an RSVP from him! She was shocked that he'd want to come to her humble party, but worried at the same time that she wouldn't have enough food to feed everyone.

Karen was the first to reach the door and Emily greeted her.

"I've brought one of my oregano and sun-dried tomato loaves," Karen said, handing her a basket that smelled delicious.

"Oh, Karen, you shouldn't have," Emily said, taking the basket.

"It's actually a business tactic," Karen said in a hushed tone out the corner of her mouth. "If this group likes them, they'll be coming to the general store to stock up!" She winked.

Emily smiled and stepped aside to let her in. She hadn't been sure about Karen, but it seemed like the woman's usual friendliness had returned.

Emily then turned to face the mayor. She nodded courteously and held out her hand to shake.

"Thank you for coming," she said.

The mayor took one look at her hand, then reached past it and pulled her into a tight embrace. "I'm just glad you're finally opening your heart to our little town."

At first Emily felt uncomfortable being hugged by the mayor like that, but his words touched her and she relaxed.

Finally, all the guests were in the house, mostly congregated in the living room, and Emily had a chance to socialize with them.

"I was just telling Rico here," Birk said to her, "that you should think about turning this place back into a B&B."

"I didn't know it used to be one," Emily replied.

"Oh yes, before your dad bought the place it was," Rico said. "I think it was a B&B from 1950 to sometime in the eighties."

Serena laughed and patted Rico's hand. "He can't remember my name but he remembers that," she said out the corner of her mouth.

Emily laughed.

"I bet it paid for itself," Birk added. "And just the sort of place this town needs."

The more she spoke to people, the more Emily realized how gracious they were. The idea of her turning the house into a B&B seemed to spread like wildfire, and the more she thought about it, the better an idea it seemed to her as well. It had, in fact, been a dream of hers when she was younger to work in a B&B, but after becoming a surly teenager she'd lost confidence in her ability to connect with people. Her dad's abandonment had hit her hard, had knocked her for a loop, and she'd been guarded and hostile ever since. But the town had softened her. Maybe she did still have it in her to be a gracious hostess?

It was time for dinner so Emily shepherded everyone into the dining room. There were lots of gasps and cries of admiration as everyone wandered in and took in the sight of the renovated room.

"I won't be able to show you the ballroom, I'm afraid," Emily said. "The window was damaged in the storm so it's all boarded up again."

No one seemed to mind. They were too enthralled by the dining room. Everything was complimented, from Emily's floral centerpiece to the color of the rug to the choice of wallpaper.

"You have quite the hand for flower arranging," Raj said, sounding impressed.

"And aren't these chairs delightful?" Serena joked, running her fingers across the dining chairs she'd helped Emily source from Rico's flea market.

It took a long time to get everyone seated. Once they were, Emily went out into the kitchen to serve up. The sound of the hubbub radiating from the dining room made her feel warm and loved.

She made it into the kitchen and quickly checked on Mogsy and the pups in the utility room. They were all sleeping contently as though without a care in the world. Then she went back into the kitchen and began to serve the food.

"Want a hand carrying it all in?" Serena's voice came from the door.

"Please," Emily said. "This is bringing back terrible memories of my waitressing days."

Serena laughed and helped stack up Emily's arms until she was balancing five plates. Serena did the same, and together they went into the dining room to the sounds of delighted "oohs" and "ahs."

Emily couldn't help feeling a little frustrated. Daniel was supposed to be here to help her out. She'd thought of the dinner party as a sort of coming out party for the two of them. She wanted to see how people reacted to her being with a local, with one of them. She thought at the very least it would buy her a little bit of kudos. But Daniel had disappeared, leaving her to do everything alone.

Once everyone had a plate in front of them—and thankfully there had been just enough to feed them all—the meal began.

"Emily, your father went to a Catholic school, didn't he?" the mayor asked.

The fork that had been on its way to Emily's mouth suddenly paused. "Oh," she said awkwardly. "I don't actually know."

"I'm sure we shared a few stories of mean nuns," the mayor said quickly, sensing Emily's discomfort about talking about her father.

Cynthia, on the other hand, seemed oblivious. "Oh, your dad, Emily. He was such a great guy," she exclaimed. She had her glass high in the air. Red wine sloshed precariously close to the rim every time she gesticulated, which was often. "I remember this time, it must have been at least twelve years back now, because it was before Jeremy and Luke were born, while I still had my figure." She paused and cackled.

Emily didn't correct her that it had to have been at least twenty years, but she could tell from the awkward shuffles around the dinner table and the averted eyes that enough people were thinking it and feeling bad on her behalf.

"It was the first time he came into my store," Cynthia continued, "and he was asking for this very specific book, an old one that was out of print. I don't remember the title but it was something to do with flower fairies. Now I knew he'd moved into the house on West Street and I'd seen him a few times. Every time I'd seen him he was alone. So I'm looking at this grown man, getting a bit nervous, wondering what he wants a collector's edition book on fairies for. I keep thinking I must have misheard him and I'm leading him around the bookstore showing him all these different books with similar titles, and he's saying, 'no, no, that's not it. It's about fairies.' I didn't have it so had to order it in for him, which bumped up the price even more. He didn't seem to mind at all, so I'm thinking he's really committed to getting this collector's edition of a book on fairies. So a few weeks later the book is delivered and I call him up to say it's there for him to pick up. I'm a bit nervous, but when he comes in he's pushing this lovely little girl in a stroller. That must have been you, Emily. The relief I felt, you would not believe!"

There was a moment of silence around the table as people looked to Emily, trying to work out what would be the appropriate way to react. When they saw that she was starting to giggle, they too let their own stifled laughter out. There was almost a perceptible moment where the tension they'd been holding was released.

Cynthia finished off her anecdote. "I told him I thought you were a little too young to read the book but he said that it was for when you got older, that his mom had owned a copy and he wanted you to have one too. Isn't that just the most darling thing you ever heard?"

"Yes," Emily said, grinning. "I'd never heard that story before."

Emily felt grateful to Cynthia for giving her another beautiful memory she could cherish. It also saddened her, making her miss her dad even more.

After Cynthia's story, conversation quickly turned to the idea of turning the house into a B&B.

"I think you should do it," Sunita said. "Turn this place into a B&B. You'd be more likely to get your permit for that because it would benefit everyone in town to have one."

"True," the mayor said. "It would protect you from Trevor as well."

Emily smirked. She was getting the distinct impression that Trevor Mann was thoroughly disliked in the community, and that he in no way represented any of the people sitting around her dining table.

"Well," Emily said, sipping at her wine, "it's a lovely idea. But I only have three months' worth of money left before I go broke."

"Enough to get some of the bedrooms fixed?" Birk asked.

"That's a good point," Barbara joined in. "The dining room, living room, and kitchen are all already done. If you had a bedroom you'd have everything you needed to start you off. Voila. Bed and breakfast."

She was right. They all were. That really was all Emily needed to get her dream off the ground. Enough of the house and grounds were already to a standard that guests would enjoy. If she set the bar low—just to get one customer through the door, for example—that would be achievable just as soon as she'd renovated a bedroom. Then with a small amount of income dripping in, she'd be able to reinvest in the business, do up another room, and grow the business slowly that way.

"Well, Barbara," Karen said, "she'd need the breakfast part as well."

Everyone laughed.

"Funnily enough," Raj said, "I've actually got some chickens I need to rehome. You could take them and then you would have fresh eggs for the breakfasts!"

"And you already make the best coffee in town," the mayor added. "No offense, Joe."

Everyone looked at the diner owner.

"None taken!" he chuckled. "I know coffee isn't my strong suit. I'd be more than happy to endorse Emily's business."

"So would I," Birk said.

"And if you need any advice," Cynthia added, "I'd be more than happy to impart my wisdom. I managed a B&B when I was in my twenties. No idea how they thought I was responsible enough to do that, but the place didn't burn down on my watch, so I guess they were right!"

Emily couldn't believe what she was hearing. All these people were willing to help her out. It was an amazing feeling, and she was overwhelmed by their generosity and kind words. To think she'd been so dismissive of them when she'd first arrived here. How different things had become in just a few short months.

But her joy was diminished by one snag. Daniel. He lived on the grounds too. His life would be disrupted immeasurably if she opened a B&B. They'd lose their privacy. She couldn't do it without speaking to him first. In some way it had the potential to work out brilliantly for them. Daniel could move into the main house with her and they could rent out the carriage house as a self-contained unit, or a bridal suite, even. And the ballroom would be the perfect venue to host weddings.

Emily's mind began to run away with her. Maybe she'd had one glass of wine too many, but she was filled with a sense of optimism she hadn't felt for years. Suddenly, the future looked bright, exciting, and secure.

She just wondered why Daniel wasn't here to share the moment with her.

Chapter Fifteen

It was late, the party long over, when Emily finally heard the sound of Daniel's motorcycle coming up the street and turning onto the drive up to the house. She got out of bed and peered through the window at his figure as he removed his helmet and walked up toward the carriage house.

Emily wrapped herself up in her nightgown then slid on her slippers. She went downstairs and out the front door. The grass was soft as she walked across the lawn toward the carriage house. Light was coming from inside, spilling across the grass.

She knocked on the door then stood back, wrapping her arms around herself to keep out the chilly night air.

Daniel answered the door. Something about the look on his face told her that he already knew it would be her standing there.

"Where have you been?" she demanded. "You missed the party."

Daniel took a deep breath. "Look, why don't you come in? We can talk over tea rather than standing out here in the cold." He held the door open for her. Emily went inside.

Daniel made them both tea and Emily stayed quiet throughout, waiting for him to be the first to speak, to offer an explanation for his behavior. But he remained tight-lipped and she was left with no other options.

"Daniel," she said forcefully, "why did you miss the party? Where were you? I was worried."

"I know. I'm sorry. I just don't like those people, okay?" he said. "They're the ones who wrote me off when I was a kid."

Emily frowned. "That was twenty years ago."

"It doesn't matter if it was twenty years or twenty minutes to these people."

"You were singing their praises at the harbor," Emily said. "Now suddenly you hate them?"

"I like some of them," Daniel contested. "But they're mostly small-minded townsfolk. Believe me, it would have been worse if I'd been there."

Emily raised an eyebrow. She wanted to tell him he was wrong, that those people had turned out to be kind, fun folk. That she was beginning to consider them friends. But the last thing she wanted was to have an argument with Daniel when their honeymoon phase had barely begun.

"Why didn't you just tell me you didn't want to come to the party?" she said finally, forcing her voice to be calm. "I felt like an idiot waiting around for you."

"I'm sorry." Daniel sighed with regret, then set a cup of tea down in front of her. "I know I shouldn't have disappeared like that. It's just I'm so used to being alone, to not having anyone to answer to. It's part of who I am. Having all those people around suddenly, it's a lot to cope with all at once."

Emily felt bad for him, for the way he felt more comfortable alone. To her, that didn't seem like a particularly happy trait to possess. But it still didn't excuse his behavior.

"I mean, just Cynthia on her own would have been bad enough," Daniel added with a sheepish grin.

In spite of herself, Emily laughed. "You should have just told me," she said.

"I know," Daniel replied. "If I promise not to take off like that again, will you forgive me?"

Emily couldn't stay mad at him. "I guess," she said.

Daniel reached over and took her hand. "Why don't you tell me how it was? What did you all talk about?"

Emily gave him a look. "You want me to recount the conversations of people you just told me you hated?"

"I won't hate it coming from you," Daniel said with a smile.

Emily rolled her eyes. She wanted to stay mad at Daniel for a little bit longer to teach him a lesson, but she just couldn't help herself. Plus, she had some big news to tell him regarding the B&B and she couldn't hold it in any longer. She tried to dampen her enthusiasm but found herself unable to contain it.

"Well, the main topic of conversation," she said, "was turning the house into a B&B."

Daniel almost spat out the sip he'd taken. He looked up over the rim of his teacup. "A what?"

Emily tensed up, suddenly nervous about telling Daniel about her new dream. What if he didn't support her? He'd just told her that being alone was part of who he was, and now she was about to tell him that having all manner of strangers traipsing in through the property might become a common occurrence.

"A B&B," she said, her voice smaller and more timid.

"You want to do that?" Daniel asked, setting his cup down. "Run a B&B?"

Emily wrapped her hands around her own cup as though for reassurance and shifted in her seat. "Well... maybe. I don't know. I mean I'd need to crunch the numbers first. I probably won't even be able to afford to get it off the ground." She was stammering now, trying to downplay the idea, unsure what Daniel would make of it.

"But if you could afford to, that's what you'd want?" he asked.

Emily looked up and met his eye. "It was what I wanted to do when I was younger. It was my dream, actually. I just didn't think I'd be any good at it so I gave up thinking about it."

Daniel reached out and put his hand over hers. "Emily, you'd be amazing at it."

"You think so?"

"I know so."

"So you don't think it's a terrible idea?"

Daniel shook his head and beamed. "It's a great idea!"

She brightened suddenly. "You really think so?"

"Absolutely," he added. "You'd be an amazing host. And if you need money to put into it I'd be happy to help. I don't have much but would give you whatever I have."

Though touched by his offer, Emily shook her head. "I couldn't take your money, Daniel. All I'd really need to get things started is one decent bedroom and a pot of coffee. Once I get the first guest in, I can put the profit straight back into the business."

"Even so," Daniel said. "If you need any renovation work done, work on the grounds and stuff, you know I'm happy to chip in."

"Really?" Emily asked again, still unable to believe it. "You'd do that for me?" She thought again of Daniel's generosity, and how he came through for her in her time of need. "You really think it's a good idea?"

"Yes," Daniel assured her. "I love the idea. Which bedroom would you do up first?"

During their last three months of doing up the property they hadn't made much headway with the upstairs. It was only Emily's parents' old room (now hers) and the bathroom that had been completed. She'd need to select another one of the rooms to focus on.

"I don't know yet," Emily said. "Probably one of the big ones at the back."

"One with an ocean view?" Daniel suggested.

Emily gave a little shrug. "I'd have to put a bit more thought into it first. But it wouldn't take long to fix up, would it? I could have it ready for the tourist season. If I got a permit, that is."

Daniel seemed to be in agreement. Over their cup of tea they went over all the details, the amount of time and money they'd need to get a room ready and a menu together in time for the summer influx of tourists.

"It would be risky," Daniel said, sitting back and looking at the paper in front of him scrawled with figures and sums.

"It would," Emily agreed. "But then again quitting my job and walking out on my boyfriend of seven years was risky and look how well that played out." She reached forward and squeezed Daniel's arm. As she did so, she sensed a hesitation in him. "Is everything okay?" she asked, frowning.

"Yeah," Daniel said, standing and picking up their empty mugs. "I'm just tired. I think I'll call it a night."

Emily stood too as it suddenly dawned on her that he was asking her to leave. The passion of the previous evenings seemed to have been entirely extinguished. The romance of their morning in the rose garden dispersed. The thrill of the motorcycle ride across the cliff tops gone.

Pulling her nightgown tightly around her, Emily went over and kissed Daniel on the cheek. "See you later?" she asked.

"Uh-huh," he replied, not looking her in the eye.

Bewildered and hurt, Emily left the carriage house and made the cold, lonely walk back to her own house to spend the night alone.

*

"Morning, Rico!" Emily called as she strolled into the dark, over-crammed indoor flea market the next day.

Instead of Rico, it was Serena's head that popped up from behind a table that she was in the middle of artfully distressing. "Emily! How's it going with Mr. Hot Stuff? I never got a chance to properly talk to you about it at the party."

Daniel was about the last thing Emily wanted to talk about at that point in time. "If you'd asked me that two days ago I would have said it was going amazingly. But now I'm not so sure."

"Oh?" Serena said. "He's one of those, is he?"

"One of what?"

"Falls in too deep and scares themselves cold. I've seen it a million times."

Emily wasn't sure how a twenty-year-old could have seen anything a million times but didn't say it. She didn't really want to get into a conversation about Daniel right now.

"So, I'm looking for a couple of specific pieces," Emily said, rummaging in her bag for the list she and Daniel had made last night before he'd effectively kicked her out his house. She handed it to Serena. "I'm not ready to buy anything yet, I just want to get some ballpark figures."

"Sure," the younger woman said, beaming. "I'll just have a look around." She was about to head off into the shop when she paused. "Hey, this is all bedroom stuff. Is it…"

"For a B&B?" Emily smiled and wiggled her eyebrows. "Yup."

"That's so cool!" Serena exclaimed. "You're really going to do it?"

"Well," Emily said, "I'll need to get the permit first, which means going to a town meeting."

"Oh pfft, that'll be easy," Serena said, waving a dismissive hand. "Does this mean you won't be going back to New York?"

"I need to get the permit first," Emily repeated with a slightly sterner tone.

"Got it," Serena said, clicking her fingers. "Permit first." She grinned and walked away.

Emily smiled to herself, happy to know there was at least one person who seemed to genuinely want her to stick around in Sunset Harbor, not just because of the profit she'd bring to the area but because they liked her.

She went over to the drawer of door handles and started looking through it. Rico had a collection to rival her father's, though Rico's were in much better condition. She was considering powder blue for the color scheme of the room, and wanted delicate glass handles to go in the chest of drawers.

As she was rummaging through the drawer of handles and knobs, she heard two voices entering the shop behind her.

"Stella said she saw him up on the cliffs again yesterday, riding his motorbike for hours and hours," one of the voices said.

Emily paused and strained to hear them better. Could they be talking about Daniel? He had a penchant for driving his bike on the cliffs, and he had been gone for a really long time yesterday.

"And he was at the festival down at the harbor the other day," the second voice said.

Emily felt her heart rate increase. Daniel had been at the festival. Well, so had everyone else, but not everyone else rode a

130

motorbike along the cliff path. She felt certain they were gossiping about Daniel.

"You don't think he's moved back into town, do you?" the second voice was saying.

"Well, Stella has a theory that he never left," the first said.

"Oh my. Really? Just the thought of it gives me the chills. You mean to say he's been at the old house this whole time?"

"Yes, exactly. Stella told me that someone told her that he was at the garage sale the new girl had up there the other day."

Emily felt her whole body turn to ice as the voices kept on gossiping.

"Really? Goodness me. Someone ought to warn her!"

Certain now that the women were talking about Daniel, Emily stepped out of the shadows. "Warn me about what?" she said coolly.

The two women stopped and stared at her like rabbits caught in the headlights.

"I said," Emily repeated, "warn me about what?"

"Well," the first woman began, her voice now suddenly trembling. "It was Stella that said that she'd seen him."

"Seen who?"

"The Moreys' son, I forget his name. Dustin. Declan."

"Douglas," the other woman informed the first confidently.

"No, it's more exotic than that. More unusual," the first contested.

Emily folded her arms and raised an eyebrow. "It's Daniel. And what about him?"

"Well," the first woman said, "he has a reputation."

"A reputation?" Emily said.

"With women," she added. "He's left a lot of women with broken hearts, that Declan."

"Douglas," the second woman said.

"*Daniel*," Emily corrected them both.

The first woman shook her head. "It's not Daniel, dear. I can't remember his name but it's definitely not Daniel."

"I'm telling you, it's Douglas," the second woman said.

Emily was starting to get frustrated. She didn't want to believe what the women were saying about Daniel—about the women in his past—but she couldn't help the niggling doubt that they were creating in her mind. "Look, I'm sure that was all a very long time ago. People change. Daniel isn't like that anymore and I'm not getting into this argument with you. You should mind your own business, okay?"

The first woman frowned. "It's not Daniel! Honestly, girl, I've been in this town a damn sight longer than you have. That boy's name is not Daniel."

The second woman clapped her hands. "I've got it. Dashiel."

"Yes that's it! Dashiel Morey."

Just then Serena reappeared. She paused mid-stride when she saw the two elderly women standing there and Emily looking flustered.

"I have to go," Emily said, turning and striding out of the shop.

"Wait, what about your list?" Serena called out as Emily disappeared.

As soon as she was out in the springtime sunshine, Emily bent over and began to take deep breaths. She felt like she was hyperventilating. Her mind seemed to be spinning in circles. Though she knew the old women were just busybodies, she couldn't help but feel rattled by what they'd said, by how certain they were about Daniel's name, about his past indiscretions with women. And though Emily had been with Daniel mind, body, and soul, she had the sudden, dreadful realization that she didn't really know him at all, that one couldn't really ever truly know a person anyway. Her dad had taught her that much. If a loving family man could walk out on his family never to be seen again, then a guy she'd known for a few months could be lying about his name.

And his intentions.

Chapter Sixteen

Emily drove home quickly, her vision blurring with tears. She didn't want to overreact but she really had no other option. Daniel had lied to her about the most fundamental part of his being: his name. What kind of a person did that? Even if he had changed his name because he hated it or was embarrassed by it, that was the sort of thing Emily would expect to crop up in conversation at some point. She didn't go by *her* full name of Emily Jane but she'd still spoken about it to Daniel and even then, in that specific conversation about names, Daniel hadn't piped up and said anything. Which led her to believe it was because he was deliberately hiding his identity from her.

And if he could lie to her about that, then maybe what the women had said about the string of broken hearts he'd caused could be true as well.

As she pulled up to the house, Emily saw that Daniel was in the yard, tending to the shrubs. He looked up, frowning, at the sound of her speedy approach and the squealing brakes as she slammed the car to a halt. She parked the car carelessly at a strange angle, then sprang out from the passenger seat, leaving it with its engine running and the door wide open. Then she stormed across the lawn heading right for Daniel.

"Who are you?" she cried, jabbing him in the chest as she reached him.

Daniel staggered back, looking shocked and confused. "What the hell kind of question is that?"

"Tell me!" Emily yelled. "Your name isn't Daniel, is it? It's Dashiel. Dashiel Morey."

A crease formed between Daniel's eyebrows. "How—"

"How did I find out?" Emily cried in an accusatory manner. "I had to hear it from two old women in the flea market. Because you didn't have the guts to tell me yourself. Do you know how humiliating that was for me?" She could feel her blood boiling at the mortifying memory.

"Emily, look I can explain," Daniel said, bringing his hands to her shoulders.

Emily shoved his hands off from her shoulders. "Don't touch me. You've been lying to me this whole time. It's true. Just tell me straight Your name really is Dashiel?"

"Yes. But it's just my name that's changed. It's—"

"I can't believe this. And the women? That's all true too, isn't it!" She threw her hands up exasperated.

"Women?" Daniel asked, frowning.

"All those hearts you broke! You have a reputation, Daniel. Or should I say Dashiel?" She turned away, tears pricking at her eyes. "I don't even know who you are anymore."

Daniel exhaled with emotion. "Yes you do, Emily. I'm exactly the same person I always was."

"But WHO is that?" Emily cried, bringing her finger up to his face. "A violent criminal who puts people in hospitals? A sensitive photographer running away from home? Some lothario who uses women up then discards them when he's done with them? Or are you just the silent, stammering caretaker who is freeloading off me?"

Daniel's mouth dropped open and Emily knew she'd pushed it too far. But she couldn't stand to be deceived, by Daniel of all people, after everything they'd been through together. She'd shared so much with him—her dreams, her pain, her past, her bed. She'd trusted him, perhaps naively so.

"That's below the belt," Daniel shot back.

"I want you off my land," Emily shouted. "Out of my carriage house. Get out! Take your stupid motorcycle with you!"

Daniel just stared at her, his expression somewhere between appalled and disappointed. Emily had never thought she'd see him look at her that way. It felt like a dagger to the heart to see that look in his eyes, to know it was directed at her and that her cruel words had caused it.

Daniel didn't utter another word. He walked calmly to the garage and wheeled out his bike. Then he gunned it to life, gave her one last, stony stare, and drove off.

Emily watched him go, her hands held in tight fists, her heart beating wildly, wondering if that was going to be the last time she would ever see him.

*

Emily trudged wearily back into the house. The argument with Daniel had taken it out of her, exhausted her. She desperately wanted to speak to Amy, but had recently gotten the feeling that her friend was growing exasperated with her. Their text exchanges had become shorter, less frequent, and days would pass without hearing from her. If she called her now with woes about a man she hadn't even gotten around to telling Amy she was dating, that would probably be the nail in the coffin for their friendship.

As she walked through the corridor, she felt like everything had been tainted by Daniel. The splotch of paint on the floorboards beside the staircase from when they'd been painting the hall and he'd sneezed. The slightly crooked picture frame they'd spent the good part of an hour trying to get straight before giving up and concluding that it simply had to be the wall that was wonky, not the frame. Everywhere she turned, she had a memory of Daniel. But right now Emily wanted space from him, not just physically but mentally. And that's when it occurred to her that there was one room in the house that she had not yet set foot in, that was not tainted by Daniel. One room that had remained perfectly preserved, not just for the last twenty years but for twenty-eight years. And that was the bedroom she and Charlotte had shared.

Emily climbed the stairs now, filled with anguish. Ever since she'd arrived here she'd been avoiding the room. It was a habit she'd picked up from her parents, who never went in there again after Charlotte's death. They'd immediately moved Emily into another room in the house, had shut the door to the room that reminded them of their deceased child, and had simply never opened it again. As if it were that easy to eradicate the pain of her death.

Emily walked right down the corridor and went up to the door. She could see faint scratches and dents on the wood from when she and her sister would carelessly slam the door running through while playing tag. She rested her hand against it, wondering if now was a bad time to do this since she was already in a fragile state, or whether she was going inside as a sort of punishment to herself, a way of causing self-inflicted pain. But she wanted to be close to her sister. Charlotte's death had robbed her of having someone to confide in. She'd never been able to talk to her about boy troubles or relationship woes. Now she felt like this would be the closest she could get to her sister. And so she gripped the door handle, twisted it, and stepped over the threshold into a room that had been preserved in time.

Walking into that room was like unearthing a time capsule or stepping into a family photograph. Emily was immediately hit with an overwhelming sense of nostalgia. Even the smell of it, though hidden beneath the aroma of dust, brought back memories and feelings she had all but forgotten. She was unable to hold back her tears. A great sob ripped out of her and she clutched her mouth as she took a small step forward into the room containing all those precious memories of her sister.

The girls had been given the biggest room of the house. There was a mezzanine at one end and huge floor to ceiling windows at the other with a view over the ocean. Emily had a flash of memory of making her dolls climb the ladder to the mezzanine, pretending it was a mountain and they were intrepid explorers. Emily smiled mournfully to herself at the memory of a time long past.

She paced around the room, picking up items that had remained untouched for almost three decades. A coin bank in the shape of a bear. A plastic neon pink toy pony. She couldn't help but let out a laugh at all the garish toys she and Charlotte had filled the room with. It must have driven her mom crazy that her daughters were in the most beautiful, stylish room of the house and had filled it with rainbow octopuses. Even the wooden dollhouse in the corner had been covered in stickers and glitter.

There was a large built-in wardrobe on one side of the room. Emily wondered whether their dress-up princess outfits were still inside. They had all the Disney ones. Her favorite had been the Little Mermaid and Charlotte's had been Cinderella. Emily went over and opened the wardrobe door. When she looked inside she discovered that all of Charlotte's outfits were still hanging there, untouched since her death.

Suddenly, looking at the clothes caused Emily to have another flashback. But this one was so much more vivid than the scraps of memory that had come back to her as she'd walked around the room. This flashback felt real, immediate, and dangerous. She gripped the wall to steady herself as she saw, with clarity, the moment when her clasp on Charlotte's hand had slipped and the little girl had disappeared, her bright red raincoat swallowed up by the gray rain.

"No!" Emily cried, knowing how the story ended and desperately wanting to stop the inevitable, the moment when her sister fell into the water and drowned.

Then suddenly the vision was over and Emily was back in the bedroom, her palms slick with sweat, her heart racing a mile a minute. She looked down to find that she was tightly gripping the sleeve of that very same raincoat; its polka dot design was unmistakable. She must have gripped it during the terrifying memory.

Wait, Emily thought suddenly, looking at the tiny red raincoat in her grasp.

136

She scrabbled around in the wardrobe and found Charlotte's boots with a ladybug design.

Emily had always believe that Charlotte had fallen into the water and drowned because she'd let go of her hand in that storm. But here were her clothes. Unless her mom had had them dry cleaned after Charlotte's body had been returned to them, then put them back in the wardrobe along with all of her other clothes, Charlotte must have come home that day, alive and safe. Could it be that Emily had conflated two events in her mind? That the death of Charlotte had come after the storm? Had been caused by something else?

In a flash, Emily ran out of the room and downstairs to where her cell phone was in its usual perch by the front door. She grabbed it, scrolled through the numbers, and dialed her mom. The sound of ringing filled her ear.

"Come on, pick up," she muttered under her breath, willing her mom to answer.

At last, she heard the static noise that indicated the call had connected, and then she heard her mom's voice for the first time in months.

"I was wondering when you'd pick up the phone and apologize to me about running away from New York."

"Mom," Emily stammered. "That's not why I'm calling. I need to talk to you about something."

"Let me guess," her mom said, sighing. "You need money. Is that it?"

"No," Emily said forcefully. "I need to talk to you about Charlotte."

There was a long, heavy silence on the other end of the phone.

"No you don't," her mom said, finally.

"Yes I do," Emily insisted.

"It was a long time ago," her mom said. "I don't want to drag up the past."

But Emily wasn't going to let her make excuses anymore. "Please," she pleaded. "I don't want to never speak about her. I don't want to forget. It's not like we have anyone else."

At this, her mom seemed to soften. But she was as blunt as she ever was. "What made you decide you suddenly wanted to talk about her?"

Emily chewed her lip, knowing her mom wouldn't like the answer. "It was Dad, actually. He left a letter for me."

137

"Oh, did he now?" her mom said, the bitterness in her voice unmistakable. "How very nice of him." Emily tried not to feed into her mom's anger. She didn't want to get into *that* old argument about her dad. "And what did the letter say about Charlotte?"

Emily shifted from foot to foot. Even after months away from her nonplussed mom, the old need to please her resurfaced, making Emily feel anxious and agitated. It took her a while to formulate her sentence, to get out the words she needed to say.

"Well, he said it wasn't my fault that Charlotte died."

There was another long pause from the other end of the line. "I didn't know you thought it was your fault."

"Why would you?" Emily said. "We never spoke about it."

"Because I didn't think there was anything to talk about," her mom said defensively. "It was an accident and she died and that was that. What on earth could have given you the impression that you were in any way to blame?"

Emily felt her mind swirling again. It felt so alien to be engaged in this conversation with her mom after so many years of silence, and so many months of estrangement. She felt a shard of pain lodge in her throat as tears found their way into her eyes. "Because I let go of her hand in the storm," she stammered through her sobs. "I lost her and then she drowned in the ocean."

Her mom exhaled loudly. "It wasn't the ocean, Emily. That wasn't how she died."

Emily felt like her world was crashing down around her. Everything she'd believed to be true was shattering. Not only had Daniel betrayed her trust, but now she couldn't even trust her own memories?

"Then how did she die?" Emily asked in a quiet, nervous voice.

"You really don't remember?" her mom asked, sounding shocked and bemused in equal amounts. "Emily, your sister drowned in the swimming pool. It was nothing to do with you or the storm."

"Swimming pool?" Emily repeated in a daze.

But no sooner had the words left her lips than a swarm of memories hit Emily in a flurry. She dropped the phone and ran to her father's study. There she grabbed the key chain she'd found in the vault, with all its many keys. She raced through the house, the noise of her heavy footsteps distressing the puppies and making them yap in anger.

She ran straight out the front door without bothering to put her shoes on, and up to the barn. Raj had removed the fallen tree from its roof, so she just had to step over the broken planks to get inside. She went past the destroyed darkroom and the boxes that contained the rain-ruined remains of Daniel's photographs, then up to the door she'd seen the first time she was in here, the door to nowhere. She fumbled with the chain, trying one key after the other, until she found one that fit the lock, turned it and pushed the door open.

It swung open and hit the side, making a bang echo out. Emily peered into the new, undiscovered room. And there it was. The large empty swimming pool in which Charlotte had drowned, and in doing so, changed the course of Emily's life forever.

She could see her now, her little sister dressed in her Care Bear pajamas, face down in the water. The memories came back to her with the force of a tsunami.

Her parents had told them they were getting a pool put in the summer house. She and Charlotte had kept trying to guess where the pool would be, had tried sneaking into different rooms looking for it, then had finally found it in the outbuilding. Charlotte had wanted to swim right away, but Emily knew they wouldn't be allowed to without supervision and had reminded her little sister to keep it a secret that they'd found the pool. That evening their mom went out and their dad fell asleep on the sofa. Charlotte must have gotten out of bed to secretly swim. Something had woken Emily, maybe the unusual silence from the lack of Charlotte snoring in the bed beside her. She'd gone looking for her and found her in the pool. It had been Emily who'd had to rouse her father from his drunken stupor.

Emily shook her head, feeling suddenly nauseous She didn't want to believe it. Was that why she had no memory? Because seeing her dead sister had traumatized her so much she'd blocked it out entirely? And her mind, in attempting to fill in the blanks, had turned the guilt she felt at being the one to rouse her father into a different type of guilt, into blame?

It hadn't been the storm. It hadn't been her fault. She had lived under a cloud of guilt for all these years for no reason—just because she'd learned from her parents to ignore her problems, to forget the things she did not like about her past. Because of them she'd repressed the trauma of finding Charlotte floating face down and lifeless in the pool twenty-eight years ago, and her mind had tried to fill in the blanks, to explain Charlotte's absence, picking the memory that made the most sense.

It really wasn't her fault.

Emily collapsed to her knees at the edge of the pool and cried.

It was the sound of Mogsy's frantic barking that finally brought Emily back to her senses. She looked up, not sure how long she had been sitting there at the side of the pool staring into the emptiness, but when she stood up and went back into the barn, the sky she could see through the hole in the roof was black. Stars winked down at her and the moon was hazy. That's when Emily realized it was obscured by smoke. She sniffed and smelled burning.

Heart racing, Emily rushed through the barn and out onto the lawn. She could see the house ahead and smoke billowing from the kitchen window. Mogsy and the puppies were barking from inside.

"Oh God, no," she cried aloud as she ran across the grass.

When she got to the kitchen door, she went to reach out for the door handle when a sudden force shoved her out of the way. She stumbled then looked up. It was Daniel, suddenly appearing out of nowhere.

"Did you do this?" she screamed, terrified that he'd committed arson out of revenge.

Daniel stared at her, horrified by the accusation. "If you open the door you'll create a suction draft. The flames will race toward the oxygen. Toward you. I was saving your life!"

Emily was too panicked to feel guilty yet. All she could think was that her house was on fire and the puppies were trapped inside, their shrill barks echoing in her ears. Through the kitchen window she could see orange flames dancing upward.

"What do we do?" she cried, grasping her hair with panic, her mind blanking.

Daniel ran to the hose that was attached to the side of the house for watering the lawn. He twisted the handle and water began to gush from the end of it. Then he smashed the window in the kitchen door with his elbow and ducked as the flame was drawn toward the source of oxygen, shooting out above him. He put the hose through the window and blasted the flame with water.

"Go to the carriage house," he shouted to Emily. "Call the fire department."

Emily couldn't believe this was happening. Her mind was swirling, filled with confusion and terror. Her house was on fire. After all the work they'd put into it, the whole thing was literally going up in flames.

She made it to the carriage house and pulled the door open. She grabbed the phone and just about managed to pump 9-1-1 into it.

"Fire!" she shouted when the call connected to the emergency operator. "West Street!"

As soon as she'd relayed that information she ran back to the house. Daniel was nowhere to be seen and the door was wide open. Emily realized he'd gone inside.

"Daniel!" she screamed, terror taking hold of her. "Where are you?"

Just then, Daniel emerged through the smoke, carrying the basket of yapping puppies, Mogsy rushing along at his heels.

Emily fell to her knees and scooped the puppies up in her arms, so relieved that they were okay. They were soot-stained. She grabbed Rain and wiped the ash from his eyes, then did the same with the other pups. Mogsy licked her face and wagged her tail as though she possessed the ability to understand the gravity of the situation.

Just then Emily saw flashing lights reflected in the glass. She turned back to see the fire truck screaming along the usually quiet street. It came right up to the house, then the fire officers inside leapt out and sprang into action.

"Is there anyone inside the property?" one of them asked her.

She shook her head and watched, stunned into silence, as they ran in through the kicked open kitchen door.

Daniel came up tentatively beside her. She looked across at him, at his ash-filled hair and soot-stained clothes.

"I'd only just fixed that damned door," he said.

Emily let out a half sob, half laugh. "Thank you for coming back," she said quietly.

Daniel just nodded. They turned back to the house and watched silently as the cloud of smoke turned into nothing more than a thin plume.

A few moments later, the fire officers emerged from the house. The lead one walked up to Emily.

"What happened?" she asked him.

"Looks like you had a faulty toaster," he said, holding up the mangled object.

"Is there much damage?" She braced herself for the news.

"Just smoke damage caused by the melting plastic. You might want to air the place out for a while. The smoke is toxic."

Emily was so relieved to hear that the house had only suffered some minor smoke damage that she threw her arms around the fireman's neck. "Thank you!" she cried. "Thank you so much!"

"Just doing my job, Emily," he replied.

"Wait, how do you know my name?" Emily asked, taken aback.

"From my dad," the fireman replied. "He's very fond of you."

"Who's your dad?"

"Birk from the gas station. I'm Jason, his eldest. You know next time you have a party, invite me too, won't you? I don't think Dad's had as much fun in all his life as he did that night. If you're that good a hostess, I want in."

"I will," Emily replied, a tad stunned by the events of the evening, and the way everyone knew everyone in this small town.

Emily and Daniel stood and watched the engine drive away, then went inside to assess the damage. Other than the stench, a black smudge running up the wall, and a melted rectangle on the countertop, the kitchen was fine.

"I can pay for the broken window," Daniel said.

"Don't be silly," Emily replied. "You were helping."

"It was hardly a fire at all. I overreacted. I just didn't want Mogsy and the puppies to choke on the smoke." He picked up Mogsy and rubbed her behind the ears and she rewarded him by licking his nose.

"You did the right thing," she added. "Fires can spread quickly. Thanks to the hose you caught it before it spread." She looked at Daniel, at his bowed head and stooped shoulders. "What made you come back?" she asked.

Daniel chewed his lip. "You didn't give me the chance to explain myself. I wanted to clear my name."

After everything he had done for her, Emily owed him that much. "Okay. Go for it. Clear your name."

Daniel pulled up a chair and sat down at the kitchen table. "Dashiel is the name I was born with," he began. "But it was also my father's name. I was named after him. So I had it legally changed when I walked out of his house because I didn't want to become a deadbeat alcoholic like he was."

Emily shifted uncomfortably. Her own father had drunk often. Was that another thing she and Daniel shared in common?

"Those people in town," Daniel continued. "They remember me as Dashiel because they want me to be bad. They want me to turn into him. To become bad." He shook his head.

Emily felt herself shrink in her seat with embarrassment. "And what about the women?"

He shrugged. "We all have past relationships, don't we? I don't think I've had more than would be normal for a young guy in this day and age. Those women are probably suspicious because I never married, you know? They think I'm a lothario because I dated, had some long-term relationships but never settled down. I'm not a monk, Emily. I have had past lovers. But I think you'd be more confused if I hadn't!"

"That's true," she said, feeling even more remorseful. "I'm sorry I let them get to me. That I let them convince me you were a bad guy."

"Do you see now that I'm not? That I'm not that guy who puts people in the hospital? Who can't take any responsibility and flunks out? Who would be stringing you along romantically and setting fire to your house?"

When he said it aloud, it did sound kind of ludicrous. "I see that now," she said in a sheepish voice.

"And you DO know who I am. I'm the guy who sat with you one night in a storm nursing a puppy back to health. Who took you to a secret rose garden on a warm spring day. Who bought you cotton candy. Who kissed you and made love to you."

He reached out for her hand. Emily looked at it, the palm open and inviting, then slid her hand in his and interlaced her fingers with his.

"Don't forget that you're also the guy who saves me from a fiery inferno," she added.

Daniel smiled and nodded. "Yes. I'm that guy too. A guy who would never want to hurt you."

"Good," Emily said. She leaned in and kissed him tenderly. "'Cause I kinda like that guy."

Chapter Seventeen

That night, Emily and Daniel rekindled their relationship, the drama of the day all but forgotten between the bed sheets, forgiveness coming in the form of caresses, ill feelings kissed away.

When morning arrived, shining a bright summer light in through the curtains, they both stirred awake.

"I guess I won't be making you breakfast," Daniel said. "Now that the toaster's exploded."

Emily groaned and let her head fall back against the pillow. "Please don't remind me."

"Come on," Daniel said. "Let's go to Joe's for breakfast." He leapt out of bed and pulled on his jeans, then extended his hand out for Emily to take.

"Can't we sleep in a little longer?" Emily replied. "It was a very trying evening if you recall."

Daniel shook his head. He seemed far too energetic for so early in the morning. "I thought you wanted to run a B&B," he exclaimed. "You won't be having many lie-ins when you're a hostess."

"Which is precisely why I need them now," Emily said.

Daniel plucked her out of bed, Emily squealing with laughter, and plopped her onto the stool by the dresser.

"Oh, looks like you're up now anyway," Daniel said with a cheeky grin. "May as well get dressed."

Once Emily was dressed, Daniel drove her to Joe's. They both ordered coffee and waffles, then got to work going through Emily's figures. She'd always been terrified of going broke and if she really did decide to give the B&B idea a go, she'd need to use all her savings. Her three-month buffer would be gone entirely. If this went wrong, she'd be left with nothing. Looking at the list of things she'd need to buy was daunting. From the ludicrously expensive things like getting the Tiffany window in the ballroom restored, to the cheap ones like replacing the blown-up toaster, Emily wasn't sure she'd be able to do it.

She threw her pen down. "It's too much," she said. "It's too expensive."

Daniel reached out and picked up the pen. He crossed the cheapest thing off the list, the toaster.

"Why did you do that?" Emily asked frowning.

"'Cause I'm going to go into the department store after breakfast and buy you a new one," he said.

"You don't have to do that."

"You're right. I want to."

"Daniel—" she warned.

"I have savings," he replied. "And I want to help you."

"But I should sell off the antiques first before you start making sacrifices for me."

"Do you really want to do that?" Daniel asked. "To sell your dad's treasures?"

She shook her head. "No. The sentimental value is too much."

"Then let me help." He squeezed her hand. "It's just a toaster."

She knew Daniel couldn't be particularly rich. Although the carriage house was decorated tastefully, he'd been living there without paying rent for twenty years. He hadn't received any money from working the grounds at the house and had probably only held down a few repair jobs here and there, just to get gas and food money and logs for the burner. Although it made her uncomfortable to know that Daniel was going to take money out of his savings, she nodded.

"And you never know," Daniel said. "People in the town could probably help. My friend George said he'd come and look at the Tiffany window and see what he could do about restoring it."

"He did?"

"Sure. People like to help out. They also like money. Maybe some of the townsfolk would invest in you."

"Maybe," Emily said. "Though they'd have no reason to."

Daniel shrugged. "Raj had no reason to chop down that fallen tree for you but he did it all the same. Some people just like to help out."

"But who around here would even have that kind of money?"

"What about Rico?" Daniel suggested, taking a swig of coffee. "I bet he's sitting on a whole hoard of cash."

"Rico?" Emily exclaimed. "He can barely remember my name." She sighed, feeling deflated and anxious. "Really, the only person with any kind of wealth is Trevor Mann. And we all know how he feels about me."

"Probably a whole lot worse than he did before thanks to the midnight visit from the fire truck."

Emily groaned and Daniel squeezed her arm to reassure her.

"I'm not going to lie, Emily," he said. "Doing this would be a huge risk. But I'm here to help, and I'll bet the rest of the town is

145

too. Do what you think is right, but know whatever you decide, you won't be alone."

Emily smiled, her fingers gently stroking down the length of his arm, reassured by his words.

"If you could get some investment," he said, "what would be the first thing you'd do with the place?"

Emily thought long and hard. "I'd want a different front desk. The foyer looks too empty at the moment."

"Oh yeah?" Daniel said. "What would you put in, in an ideal world, if money were no object?"

"Well, it would need a bespoke piece really," Emily said, picking up her cell phone and starting to search on Google and eBay. "Something like this!" she said, showing him the screen and the amazing Art Deco piece.

Daniel whistled. "That's pretty nice."

"Yup," Emily said. "And just look at the price tag. That's a good few thousand dollars out of my budget." Then she looked up and smirked at Daniel. "But if you're ever stuck for birthday gift ideas…" She put her phone back down and sighed. "Anyway, I'm getting ahead of myself. I don't even have the permit yet."

"I have every faith in you that you'll get the permit," Daniel said. Then he stood suddenly, pushing his plate away. "Come on," he said.

"Where are we going?" Emily asked.

"To Rico's. Let's see if he has anything you might want to purchase."

Emily had been reluctant to go back to Rico's, in part because the house was more or less complete, but also because of the unpleasant experience she'd had yesterday. The thought of going back in there unnerved her and she didn't feel much like reliving the moment. But with Daniel holding her hand, perhaps it wouldn't be so bad.

"We literally just did my budget! I don't have the money to buy anything fancy!" she contested.

"You know what Rico's is like. There might be some hidden gem in there somewhere."

"I doubt it," Emily replied. She'd practically scoured every inch of that place. But the idea of shopping with Daniel, of taking one small step closer to her dream, was too fun an experience to miss. Emily decided then that whatever gossip the locals had about them, she'd be able to handle it. She looked at her notebook filled with facts and figures, then snapped it shut.

"Let's go," she said.

*

"If it isn't my favorite couple," Serena said when she saw Emily and Daniel walk into the flea market. She was looking particularly stunning today in a floral sundress, stained, as usual, with multicolored paint. She kissed each of their cheeks in turn. "How's the B&B looking?"

"It looks absolutely amazing," Daniel said, wrapping an arm around Emily. "Emily's done such a great job."

Emily smiled and Serena winked at her.

"So it's done then?" she asked. "When is the grand reveal? Will you be holding another one of your parties? That stew was to die for. Ooh, that reminds me, can you write the recipe down for me, I have to send it to my mother."

"Your told your mother about my stew?"

"I tell my mother about everything," Serena said, raising an eyebrow.

Just then, Rico came out from one of the back rooms. He was looking frailer than usual, the lines on his face more pronounced.

"Hi, Rico," Emily said.

"Hello," Rico said, taking Emily's hand and shaking it. "Lovely to meet you."

"This is Emily," Serena reminded him. "Remember? We went to her house for dinner."

"Ah," Rico said. "You're the young lady with the B&B, aren't you?"

"Well, not quite yet," Emily said, smiling. "But I'm hoping to open one, yes."

"I have something for you," Rico said.

Emily, Daniel, and Serena exchanged a look.

"You do?" Emily said, confused.

"Yes, yes, I've been holding it back. This way." Rico hobbled off down the corridor. "Come on."

Shrugging, Serena followed, Daniel and Emily tagging behind with equally bemused expressions. Rico led them through a door and into a vast back room. There were lots of sheets covering large items of furniture. It felt eerie, like a graveyard of furniture.

"What's going on?" Emily whispered in Serena's ear, her first thought being that Rico had finally gone senile.

"Beats me," Serena replied. "I've never even been in here." She was looking all around her, her eyes round and intrigued. "What is all this stuff, Rico?"

"Hmm?" the old man said. "Oh, just things that are too big for the shop floor and too special to sell to anyone." He walked up to where a dust sheet was covering something large and rectangular and peeped underneath. "Yes, here it is," Rico said to himself. He began to pull the heavy dust sheet off. Emily, Daniel, and Serena sprang into action, taking corners of the dust sheet to help him.

As they pulled off the sheet, a marble surface began to emerge. Then the sheet slid fully off, revealing a gorgeous dark wooden reception desk with a marble top. It looked solid and sturdy and exactly what Emily had been looking for.

Emily gasped and looked it all over, discovering that on the other side there was a settee in red velvet attached to the piece, making it a front desk and seating area combined. It was an amazing, unique design.

"It's perfect," she said.

"This used to be in the grand foyer," Rico said.

"The grand foyer of where?" Emily asked.

"Of the B&B."

Emily's mouth dropped open. "Of my B&B? This was the original piece?"

"Oh yes," Rico replied. "Your dad absolutely loved it. He was sad to part with it but there just wasn't enough space in the house. Besides, he didn't want to do it an injustice. He wanted someone to use it as it was designed. So he gave it to me when he took on the house, hoping I'd find a buyer." He tapped the marble slab. "No one showed an interest."

It always surprised Emily when Rico spoke of the past. He seemed to have a crystal clear memory of certain events, but others he had no memory of at all. It was a stroke of luck that he'd remembered this one, and that the original front desk was exactly to Emily's taste.

But her elation was short-lived and her mood dropped. Something like this would surely cost her more than she had.

"So, how much does it cost?" she asked, bracing herself for disappointment.

Rico shook his head. "Nothing. I want you to have it."

Emily gasped. "Have it? I couldn't possibly. It must be so expensive!" She was stunned.

"Please," Rico insisted. "I haven't been able to sell it for thirty-five years. And the way your face lights up when you look at it is payment enough. I want you to take it."

Overcome with emotion, Emily threw her arms around Rico's neck and kissed his cheek. "Thank you, thank you, thank you. You have no idea what this means to me. I'll take it but it's just a loan until I get enough money together to pay you for it, okay?"

He patted her hand. "Whatever you say. I'm just happy to see it go to a loving home at last."

Chapter Eighteen

"Wake up," Daniel whispered in Emily's ear.

She stirred awake and took the cup of coffee he was offering to her, then noticed that Daniel was dressed. "Where are you going?"

"I have something to do today," he replied.

Emily looked around and noticed that the sun had barely risen. "Something? What something?"

He gave her a look. "It's a secret. But not a 'my name is actually Dashiel' kind of secret. You don't need to worry, is what I'm saying." He pressed a kiss into the crown of her head.

"Well, that's reassuring," Emily said sarcastically.

"Anyway," Daniel said, "I'd just be in your way."

"Why?" Emily asked, bleary-eyed.

Daniel raised his eyebrows. "Don't tell me you've forgotten."

"Oh my God!" Emily gasped. "The town meeting. It's today, isn't it?"

Daniel nodded. "Yup. And I think someone's having a meeting with Cynthia at seven a.m. It's currently six forty-five."

Emily leapt up. "You're right. Oh my god. I have to get dressed."

Though appreciative of Cynthia's offer to talk to her about all things B&B, she wished the woman hadn't insisted on such an early meeting time.

"That got you moving," Daniel said with a chuckle. He finished swigging his coffee, then grabbed his jacket.

"Just don't forget the meeting tonight, will you?" Emily said. "Seven p.m. at the town hall."

Daniel grinned. "I'll be there. I promise."

*

Cynthia arrived at the house with her two pet poodles in tow. She was dressed in a fuchsia pink maxi dress, the color clashing horribly with her ginger hair.

"Morning," Emily called out, waving from the door.

"Hello, sweetheart," Cynthia said. She seemed to be in a rush as she hurried up the path.

"Thanks for meeting with me," Emily added when the woman was a little closer. "Do you want some coffee?"

"Oh, I'd love some," Cynthia said.

Emily led her into the kitchen and poured them both a cup from where the pot was still brewing. As she did, Mogsy leapt up at the glass door between the kitchen and utility room. Cynthia went over and looked through the glass.

"I didn't know you had puppies!" she cried. "Oh, they're just adorable!"

"The mom was a stray," Emily said. "I didn't realize she was pregnant then suddenly there were five puppies."

"Have you found a home for them yet?" Cynthia asked, cooing through the glass at them.

"Not yet," Emily replied. "I mean the pups are too young at the moment to leave their mom. And I can't exactly kick her out to fend for herself. So for now they're mine."

"Well, once they're done weaning, I'll happily take one off your hands. Jeremy passed his entrance exams to St. Matthew's and I wanted to get him a congratulations gift."

"You'd take one?" Emily asked, feeling a sense of relief. "That would be great."

"Sure," Cynthia replied, squeezing Emily's arm. "We look out for each other in this town. Want me to ask around? See if anyone else wants one?"

"Yes, that would be amazing, thank you," Emily replied.

Emily went and fed the dogs, then the two women settled down at the table.

"Now," Cynthia said, pulling out a thick folder. "I've gone to the liberty of getting you some of the forms that you'll need to fill out. This is for hygiene." She slapped a blue piece of paper in front of Emily. Then a pink one. "Gas." Finally, she placed a yellow one on the table. "Wastewater and sewage treatment."

Emily looked at the forms with trepidation. Something about their officialness made her feel woefully under-prepared.

But Cynthia wasn't done. "I've got some business cards here for you, as well. Names and numbers of some really reputable guys. They'll get everything up to scratch for you. I used them back in the day. Good guys, the best really. I'd trust them with my life."

Emily picked the cards up and slipped them into her pocket. "Anything else?"

"Trevor's going to try to make it difficult for you. He knows the names of every code violation known to man. Make sure you know what you're doing in terms of the legal and logistical stuff and you'll be fine."

Emily gulped. She was feeling more apprehensive that ever. "And here's me thinking I just need to give a heartfelt speech."

"Oh, don't get me wrong," Cynthia exclaimed, waving one of her hands, the bright pink nails like talons. "The speech will get you ninety percent of the way there. Just don't let Trevor stump you with the other ten percent." She tapped the papers on the table. "Learn your stuff. Sound competent."

Emily nodded. "Thank you, Cynthia. I really appreciate you taking the time to speak to me about all this."

"It's no problem, hon," Cynthia replied. "We look out for each other in this town." She stood and the poodles leapt to their feet as well. "I'll see you later. Seven p.m.?"

"You're coming to the meeting?" Emily asked, surprised.

"Of course I am!" She clapped Emily on the shoulder. "We all are."

"All?" Emily asked nervously.

"All of us who care about you and the B&B," Cynthia replied. "We wouldn't miss it for the world."

Emily led Cynthia to the door, feeling a combination of grateful and apprehensive. That the people of the town would want to support her made her feel good. But to have them all watching her, and to risk making a fool out of herself in front of them, was a prospect that terrified her.

*

Later that evening, Emily was just putting the finishing touches to her outfit when she heard the doorbell ring. She frowned, confused as to who would be calling, and went to the door to see. When she opened it, she was shocked by the person she saw standing before her.

"Amy?!" Emily cried. "Oh my God!"

She pulled her friend in for a hug. Amy squeezed her back.

"Come in," Emily said, opening the door wider. She looked up at the clock quickly. There was still time to chat with Amy before she had to leave for the town meeting.

"Wow," Amy said, looking around. "This house is bigger than I expected."

"Yeah, it's kind of huge."

Amy wrinkled her nose and sniffed. "Is that smoke? I smell burning."

"Oh, long story," Emily said, waving a hand. Just then the puppies began yapping from the utility room.

"You have a dog?" Amy asked, sounding shocked.

"One dog, five puppies," Emily said. "Which is another long story." She couldn't help but glance at the clock again. "So what are you doing here, Ames?"

Amy's expression fell. "What am I doing here? I'm here to see my best friend who dropped off the radar three months ago. I mean, I should be the one asking what *you're* doing *here*. And how the hell your long weekend turned into two weeks, then *six months*. And that's not even mentioning the text I get from you saying you're thinking of starting a business!"

Emily could hear a hint of disdain in her friend's voice. "What's so crazy about the idea of me starting a business? You don't think I can?"

Amy rolled her eyes. "That's not what I meant. I just mean that things seem to be moving really fast up here. I feel like you're settling down. You have six pets!"

Emily shook her head, feeling a little exasperated, not to mention attacked. "It's a stray and her pups. I'm not settling down. I'm just experimenting. Trying things out. Enjoying my life for once."

Now it was Amy's turn to let out an exhalation. "And I'm happy for you, I am. I think it's great that you're enjoying life, you really deserve it after everything with Ben. But I just think you maybe haven't spent enough time thinking about it. Starting a business isn't easy."

"You did it," Emily reminded her.

Amy had been running a home fragrance business from home since she'd finished grad school, selling items online. It had taken her a decade of sleepless nights and seven-day work weeks to make enough money to sustain herself, but now the business was soaring.

"You're right," Amy said. "I did. And it was hard." She rubbed her temples. "Emily, if that's really what you want to do, can you at least come back to New York for a bit first, look into it properly and thoroughly? Get a business proposal together, speak to the bank for a business loan, find an accountant to help with the books? I could mentor you. Then, if you're really certain you've made the right decision, you can always come back here."

"I already know I've made the right decision," Emily said.

"How?" Amy cried. "You have zero experience! You might literally hate it! And then what? You'd have wasted all your money. You'd have nothing to fall back on."

"You know, I expect this sort of shit from my mother, Amy, not from you."

Amy sighed heavily. "It's hard to be supportive over this when you've shut me out of your life completely. I don't want to fight with you, Emily. I came here because I miss you. And I'm worried about you. This house? This isn't you. Aren't you bored here? Don't you miss New York? Don't you miss me?"

Emily's heart ached to hear the distress in Amy's voice. But at the same time, the clock on the wall told her that her time was ticking away. The town meeting would be starting shortly, a meeting that would determine her future. She needed to be there for it, and she needed to be composed.

"I'm sorry," Amy said tersely when she noticed that it was the clock on the wall where Emily's gaze kept darting. "Am I keeping you from something?"

"No, of course not," Emily said, taking Amy's hand. "It's just, can we talk about this later? I have a lot going on in my head and—"

"Me turning up unannounced was never a problem before," Amy grumbled.

"Amy," Emily warned. "You can't just disrupt my life, tell me I'm living it wrong, and expect me to be gracious about it. I'm happy to see you, I really am. And you can stay as long as you want. But right now, I have a town meeting to go to."

One of Amy's eyebrows rose. "A town meeting? For God's sake Emily, listen to yourself! Meetings are for boring backwater towns. This isn't you."

Emily lost all sense of patience. "No, you're wrong. The girl I was in New York? That wasn't me. That was some silly woman who followed Ben around like a lovesick puppy, waiting for him to tell her she was good enough to marry. I don't even recognize the person I used to be. Can't you see: this is me. Where I am now, who I am now, it's feels so much more right than New York ever did. And if you don't like it, or can't grow to support it at the very least, then we're done."

Amy's mouth dropped open. Never in all the years of their friendship had they fought like this. Never had Emily raised her voice to her oldest, closest friend.

Amy clutched her handbag tightly to her chest, then pulled a packet of cigarettes out of her purse. Her fingers moved deftly, sliding one out and placing it between her lips. "Enjoy your meeting, Emily."

She walked out of the house and to where her Benz was parked up in the street. Emily watched her speed off, her sense of regret already swirling inside of her.

Then she went to her own car, started it, and sped down the street toward the town hall, more determined than ever.

Chapter Nineteen

Sunset Harbor's town hall was a formal but quaint red-brick building. There were small trees on the lawn and a vintage wooden sign outside with gold, embossed lettering. As Emily raced up the stairs, almost dropping her folder of papers in her haste, she could almost sense the ancestors of the town watching her.

She burst in through the double doors and ran up to the reception desk, where a woman smiled at her kindly.

"Hi, I'm late for the meeting," Emily said, rummaging through her papers to find the letter that informed her what room she was supposed to be in. "I can't remember which room it was in. It's about the property on West Street."

"You must be the B&B lady," the receptionist said with a knowing smile. "Here's your name tag. The meeting's been moved to the main hall because of high level of interest. Just go through the double doors on your right."

"Thanks," Emily said, fastening her name tag to her dress and wondering what a "high level of interest" meant.

She went over to the double doors the woman had indicated and pulled them open. She was stunned to see how crammed full of people it was. A large number of the townsfolk had turned up for the discussion. She noticed the Patels, Joe from the diner, the Bradshaws, and Karen from the general store. Clearly whether her property was a B&B or not mattered to more people than she'd anticipated.

Her heart soared as she noticed Daniel right at the front. He'd come. He hadn't let her down this time. Heads swiveled as she rushed up to the front and took her seat beside him. He squeezed her knee and gave her a wink.

"You've got this," he said.

Just then, Emily saw Trevor Mann in the next aisle along peering over at her with a raised eyebrow and a sneer. She returned his cool expression with narrowed eyes.

Thankfully she'd only missed the first five minutes of the meeting. The mayor was just finishing up introducing people on the panel and running through the agenda.

"So," he said, gesturing to Emily and Trevor, "I give you the floor. Your arguments please."

Trevor didn't waste a second. He leapt up to his feet and turned to face the audience.

"I live in the property behind this house," he began. "And I am fully opposed to it being repurposed as a B&B. We already have B&Bs in the town, there's no need for one on a quiet residential street like West Street. The disruption to my life would be immense."

"Well," Emily said, her voice small, "strictly speaking you don't live on the property. It's your second home, isn't it?"

"Strictly speaking," Trevor hissed, "yours isn't your home at all."

"Touché," Emily muttered under her breath, realizing that Trevor Mann was not going to be holding anything back, certain that he would play dirty if he needed to.

She shrank back in her chair, feeling overwhelmed by the situation, listening as he rattled off statistics about noise pollution and increased refuse collections, the tourist trade and locals being priced out of the area by exactly "this sort of thing." Emily kept trying to speak but Trevor never gave her a chance. She started feeling like a gaping fish, just opening and closing her mouth.

"At the end of the day," Trevor Mann said, "we're dealing here with an inexperienced woman who doesn't know the first thing about running a business. I for one do not want the land behind my house to be used in her little vanity project."

He sat down triumphantly, expecting to hear some applause or sounds of agreement. Instead he was met by deafening silence.

"Are you going to let the poor woman speak now?" Dr. Patel said.

A cry of "Hear, hear" went up from the audience. It made Emily happy to know that the townspeople had her back. For the first time, she felt like she'd made some true friends here, something she needed at the moment what with Amy and her fighting. Thinking of Amy made the butterflies in her stomach flutter even more.

She stood up, feeling that every eye on the room was on her. She cleared her throat and began.

"First and foremost, I need you all to know how touched I am that you came. I think it's safe for me to say I wasn't very popular when I first got here. I was guarded and skeptical. But this town showed me nothing but love, warmth, generosity, and friendship. Thanks to you, I've grown to love this place, and to love all of you. I feel like I did when I came here as a girl. You've all been like parents to me, mentors, showing me how to grow into a woman. I am not looking to get rich. I just want the chance to be able to live

157

in this town, and to find a way to support myself doing it. I want the chance to fix up my father's house, which meant more to him than anything in the world. I'm not ready to leave it yet. And I also just want the chance to give back to this community."

Emily noticed all the encouraging smiles in the room. A few people were even dabbing their eyes with tissues. She continued speaking.

"The house on West Street belonged to my father. Most of you knew him. I believe, from the fond stories you've told me, that he was a cherished member of the community." She felt emotion threaten to choke her. "I miss my dad. I think you miss him too. Restoring his home feels like a way of honoring him. Turning it back into a B&B feels like a way of honoring the town he adored. All I ask is that you give me the chance to do him proud, and do you proud."

All at once, the room erupted into applause. Emily felt overjoyed by those around her, by the love and care they'd shown her once she'd been willing to let them in.

Before the clapping even had a chance to die down, Trevor Mann was back on his feet.

"How touching, Miss Mitchell," he said. "And as lovely as it is that you want to give back to the community, I have to highlight once again how grossly underqualified you are to do up a property of that magnitude, let alone successfully run a B&B."

This was it. The fight was on. And Emily was ready for it.

"Contrary to Mr. Mann's beliefs," she said, "I'm not inexperienced. I've been working on the property for months and during that time I've completely turned it around."

"Ha!" Mr. Mann called out. "She blew up the toaster just yesterday!"

Emily ignored his attempts to bring her down. "I've also obtained all the necessary permits for the work that's been done, and plans for the work that would need to be done in order to convert the property from a home into a business."

"Oh really?" Trevor sneered. "Are you telling me you've gotten plumbing and electrical permits? From licensed tradesmen?"

"Yes, I've got those," she said, pulling the forms out that Cynthia had given her.

"Well, what about your HHE-200 Sub Surface Wastewater Disposal form?" Trevor said, sounding increasingly frustrated. "Have you filled in that?"

Emily produced some more of Cynthia's documents from her folder. "Three copies, as required."

Trevor's face was beginning to turn red. "What about that barn that was damaged in the storm? You can't leave it like that, it's a hazard. But if you fix it up, it will have to comply with the land use ordinance."

"I'm well aware of that," Emily replied. "These are my construction drawings for the damaged outbuildings. And before you ask, yes, they comply with the 2009 International Building Codes. And," she continued, raising her voice to stop Trevor from interrupting, "I've had them stamped with the Maine State Architect's stamp."

Trevor scowled.

"This is all irrelevant," he finally snapped, no longer able to contain his frustration. "You are forgetting the gorilla in the room. This house was deemed uninhabitable years ago. And she has not paid her back taxes. She is living there illegally, and technically, this house is no longer even hers."

The room grew silent as all eyes turned to the mayor.

Emily's heart pounded in her throat; this was the moment of truth.

Finally, the mayor stood and faced everyone. He was trying to hide his smirk but failing miserably.

"I think we've all heard enough, haven't we?" he said. "The house was deemed uninhabitable because it was sitting empty for so many years. But we've all been through it, and it is more than inhabitable now—it is beautiful."

The crowd let out a light cheer of agreement.

"And as far as the back taxes," he continued, "Emily can pay them over time. I know our town would rather have a resident paying them off, however belatedly, than not collect any taxes at all. Besides, the new taxes and commerce a B&B would generate would much more benefit the town in the long run."

He turned to Emily and smiled wide.

"I am prepared to grant Emily the permit to convert the house into a B&B."

A cheer went up from the audience. Emily gasped, hardly able to believe what had just happened. Trevor Mann sat back in his seat, stunned into silence.

People came over to Emily, shaking her hand, kissing her cheek, clapping her on the shoulder. Emily bit her bottom lip, overwhelmed with emotion. Birk and his son Jason, the fire fighter

Emily had met, came and congratulated her. Raj Patel reminded her about the chickens he was trying to rehome.

"If you need some help with plumbing or electric, I'm eager to get on board," a man said, handing her his business card.

"Barry," she said, reading the name. "Thank you. I'll be in touch."

Karen said that if she used the general store for all her goods she'd be able to work out some kind of wholesale deal. Emily was overwhelmed by everyone's generosity and encouragement.

"When you open your B&B, I'm going to be resident artist, right?" Serena said, giving her friend a big hug.

Emily replied with a laugh.

Daniel made his way through the crowd, then swept her up into his arms and held her close to him. "I'm so proud of you."

"I can't believe it!" Emily cried, throwing her head back and laughing as he twirled her around. "We got the permit! I bet you never thought I'd get this far when you first met me."

Daniel shook his head. "To be perfectly honest, I thought you were going to do something ridiculous like leave the gas on accidentally and blow up the house. Helping you was only ever out of self-interest," he added, jokingly.

"Is that so?" Emily said, leaning in and planting a gentle kiss on his lips.

Daniel kissed her back tenderly. Emily breathed in the scent of him, thinking about how unpredictable life could really be. It hadn't been that long ago that she'd been kissing Ben, thinking she was going to marry him. How stupid she'd been. How completely different Daniel's kisses felt.

When he set her back down on her feet, Emily glanced up at him and took his hand. Amy's words were ringing in her mind, about how difficult it really was to start a business. That the majority of them failed in the first year. "Now the serious stuff starts," she said to Daniel. "The planning. The financial investment. It's a big, big risk."

Daniel nodded. "I know. But why don't we celebrate first? Just enjoy the moment."

"You're right," she said, smiling. "This is a victory. We should celebrate. But you'd better not drink too much. You need to be up early in the morning."

Daniel frowned, confused. "I do? Why?"

Emily gave him a look. "I know where you've been disappearing to," she said. "The marina."

"Oh, that," Daniel said, suddenly awkward. "What about it?"

"I've arranged for someone to deliver a new engine for your boat."

Daniel's eyes widened with surprise. "You have? But you don't have the money!"

She smiled. "You didn't have the money when you bought me the toaster but you did it anyway, just to pick me up when I was down on my luck. So I wanted to do something for you, to say thank you."

Daniel looked thrilled, and Emily knew the small financial sacrifice was worth it just for the look on his face.

"Right, this calls for Gordon's bar!" Daniel said.

Emily raised an eyebrow. "Really? You want to go out into town? What about all those busybodies and their whispering?"

Daniel just shrugged. "I don't care about them anymore. You're what's important to me." He pressed a kiss into the crown of her head.

Emily looped her arm around his waist.

As they turned to leave, she spotted someone standing at the door watching. It was Amy. Emily paused and braced herself. But instead of starting any kind of confrontation, Amy gave Emily the thumbs-up sign. Then she blew her a kiss and left.

"Who was that?" Daniel asked.

Emily smiled to herself. "Just someone from my past."

Chapter Twenty

The house was alive with people, buzzing in and out. There was lots of work to do now that the permit had been granted and it had begun immediately. So many people came forward offering their services to Emily—plastering, sanding, even window cleaning—in exchange for a company endorsement, and she was more than willing to accept their generous offers. It felt odd having so many people traipsing through the house after months of just her and Daniel. But Emily knew that she'd have to get used to it; she'd signed up for daily life intrusions when she'd decided to go ahead with the B&B.

She oversaw the delivery of the front desk Rico had donated to her. It looked incredible in the foyer. Then Barry the electrician worked downstairs installing the new till system that would sit upon it. Then Raj arrived in his white van.

"Flower basket delivery!" he said, smiling.

"Great," Emily replied.

No sooner had Raj gotten out of his van than another drove up the drive.

"We have a rug, a corridor runner for one Miss Emily Mitchell," the delivery man said, looking down at his clipboard. "Where do you want it?"

"This way," Emily replied, leading him in through the house.

Daniel was in the kitchen making coffee for everyone; she could hear him chatting with the dogs from the kitchen. Emily had managed to find homes for all the puppies except for Rain the runt and Mogsy the mother. Cynthia was taking one for her son Jeremy, Raj had agreed to give her the flower baskets for free in exchange for Thunder, the most boisterous of the puppies, Jason the firefighter was going to take one as a gift for his new baby daughter, and the final one Joe from the diner had asked for. It made Emily feel happy to know the town was once again helping her out, and she knew all the puppies would love their new homes.

Emily led the carpet deliverer up the stairs and to the landing. "Right here," she said.

She watched as he unfurled the new cream runner. It looked wonderful in the hall, perfectly complementing her gray, blue, and white color scheme.

The house was well on the way to transforming into a proper B&B and Emily began to let herself feel excited about how everything was coming together. Though her nerves were still present, they felt more like nerves of anticipation than fear. It was as though her whole life had been leading up to this moment, that she was finally where she was always supposed to be.

Emily thanked the delivery man and he left. As soon as he was gone, she walked along the soft new carpeting, trying it out like a child with a new toy. She felt thrilled, excited for the future. But then she remembered there was one very important room that she had yet to complete any renovation work on, the one that was in fact the most important. She'd been avoiding it thus far, but suddenly she felt able to go in there, to do what needed to be done.

She walked the length of the new corridor runner, past the myriad of rooms that would one day become part of the B&B but for now were empty, then stopped when she reached the closed door to the room that had once belonged to her and Charlotte. Emily laid her hands against the wood and took a deep breath. She hesitated for a moment, wondering whether she'd made the right decision after all. This was the room that had the most potential to wow, what with the mezzanine and the floor to ceiling windows with their stunning sea views. Plus, it was in the quietest part of the house. It made business sense to turn this room into the guest room. But that meant Emily couldn't delay boxing it up any longer. The success of the business hinged upon renovating this room.

Bracing herself, Emily opened the door and stepped inside. She took her time, letting it all sink in, letting the memories it held permeate her skin. Then she sat on the floor and carefully packed up all the children's books, toys, and clothes with a painful jab in her heart. As she did so, she knew that she'd made the right decision. Though boxing up her childhood hurt, ignoring what had been behind that door had been hurting her too, more than she'd realized. Perhaps now she'd be able to put that part of her life behind her and move on.

At midday the house quieted down as the workmen left for lunch. Emily stood and looked around, the last of the items in the room now boxed up and placed in their special spot in the attic, the room standing bare and empty. Tomorrow the renovation work would begin. The pink wallpaper would be stripped and the room painted white. The wood on the mezzanine was to be painted white too. Emily had already bought all the bedding and shabby chic furniture for the room, so it would just be a case of bringing it in and setting it up.

Emily sank onto the bed and stared out at the gorgeous sea view and the beautiful, cloudless sky, content in the knowledge she'd made absolutely the right decision. For once she'd put the future ahead of the past, had looked forward rather than letting herself be dragged backward. By choosing this particular room for the B&B, Emily felt like she was giving herself permission to move on with the next step of her life, that she could finally let go of the past and the misplaced guilt she felt over her sister's death.

She picked up the final box and went to take it to the attic. As she reached the door, she heard a thud and turned to see that a picture had fallen from the wall; she must have forgotten to take it down. She went and picked it up from the floor and placed it on the top of the final box. As she did so, she realized it was a picture of her and Charlotte, dressed in their raincoats, smiling broadly. In that moment, Emily felt certain it was a sign from her sister giving her permission to move on with her life.

Just then, Emily heard someone knocking on the front door. She set the last box down on the floor and went downstairs. When she opened the door, she saw that the lawn was sun-drenched. The midday sun was high in the sky, beating down on the beautiful grounds of the house, brightening the vibrant colors of the flowers Raj had planted, and the hanging flower baskets that matched.

There was a UPS man on the doorstep. "Emily Mitchell?"

"Yes, that's me," she said, taking his pen to sign for the package, excitement coursing through her as it dawned on her what had arrived.

"What's that?" Daniel asked, coming up in the hall behind her.

Emily thanked the UPS man and he strolled away. Then she turned to Daniel. "It's the sign."

"It came already?" Daniel exclaimed. "What name did you decide on?"

She'd worked in secret on the name, not wanting anyone else's influence on her decision. People kept offering her suggestions but she knew the name had to mean something to her, had to come from her and her alone.

"No peeking," she said, as she tore the wrapping off and examined the sign. It was beautiful, a blend of tasteful and rustic, which would complement the house perfectly.

With Daniel's help, she hoisted the sign into place. A thrill of excitement rippled through her as she stepped back and looked at the shiny new sign hanging proudly above the door.

"The Inn at Sunset Harbor," Daniel said, reading the sign.

"What do you think?" Emily replied.

"I love it," Daniel said, pulling her closely into him.

Just then, Emily heard the sound of crunching gravel under tires. She and Daniel turned and saw an unfamiliar car driving up along the path. It stopped in front of the house, then a man got out of the car, dragging a suitcase after him.

"Morning," he said. "The lady at the general store recommended your B&B. Do you have any vacancies?"

Emily's heart leapt with joy. She glanced quickly at Daniel and grinned, before turning back to the man and, in her most professional voice, replied:

"I think we can squeeze you in."

Coming Soon!
Book #2 in the Inn at Sunset Harbor series

Please visit www.sophieloveauthor.com to join the email list and be the first to know when it releases!

Sophie Love

A lifelong fan of the romance genre, Sophie Love is thrilled to release her debut romance series: FOR NOW AND FOREVER (THE INN AT SUNSET HARBOR—BOOK 1). Sophie would love to hear from you, so please visit www.sophieloveauthor.com to email her, to join the mailing list, to receive free ebooks, to hear the latest news, and to stay in touch!